A WORK OF HEART

THE ART OF HAVING IT ALL
BOOK THREE

SADIE WATERS

For Carter. Watch out for sofas!

CONTENTS

THREE TO GO

I reread the letter on my screen three times, trying to make sense of the offer from École des Beaux-Arts in Paris. As much as I want to text all the guys immediately and get their input, I force myself to wait, trying to take it all in and process it before I talk to any of them.

It should be an easy yes. It's what I've always wanted–the chance to live abroad, to teach, to immerse myself in a city that practically breathes art. But there's no such thing as easy when my heart belongs to four different men, and all of them are here.

When I've fully taken it in, the first person I want to talk about it with is Rafe. I already know he'll be supportive. He always is. But after all the years I've known him, I've come to truly value what he thinks and feels.

I hit call and press the phone to my ear, my nerves fluttering in my chest.

"Hey, baby," he answers, his voice lazy and warm. "Miss me already?"

I smile. "Always."

"What's up?"

I pull a blanket over my legs and curl deeper into the couch. "I just got the contract from that school in Paris."

"You mean the most prestigious art school in the world?" he teases. "Now isn't the time for modesty, baby."

"I don't feel like I deserve it," I admit. "It's a big decision. Plus, it's a whole year. In Paris."

"Which would be an amazing opportunity for you," he says, and I can almost hear the smile in his voice. "So what's the problem?"

"It's far," I complain, knowing I'm whining. "I'd miss everyone. I'd miss you."

"I'd miss you too," he says, his voice softening. "But you've gotta do what's right for you. I'm serious, Harper. This is a big opportunity. If you want it, you should take it."

My eyes burn unexpectedly. I knew he would know exactly what to say, but I didn't expect it to make me so emotional.

"Thank you, baby," I murmur.

"Hey, I'm just being honest. You'd be brilliant there."

I lean my head back against the couch and stare at the ceiling. "Would you visit me?" I ask flirtatiously.

"I was hoping you'd ask," he answers in a husky voice. "I'll even bring you real maple syrup so you don't suffer through whatever fake stuff the French think passes for pancakes."

That makes me laugh. "They don't even have pancakes, Rafe. They do crêpes."

"Even worse," he says. "See? Clearly, you'll need me there."

I grin, but my heart is still spinning like a compass needle trying to find north.

Rafe hesitates for a second before adding, "I've got something to tell you, too. Kind of big news."

"Oh?"

"I got traded."

I sit up straighter. "Again? You just went out to LA."

"Yeah. I just found out this morning. The Vikings want me back."

My heart starts pounding. "Wait," I breathe, stunned. "You're coming home?"

"That's right," he confirms, with pride dripping from his voice. "This season with the 49ers went better than expected. Minnesota saw the stats and made me an offer. Looks like I'll be back in purple and gold this fall."

I feel like I'm going to start crying again, but this time from joy. "You're really coming back to St. Paul?"

"I am," he answers in a soft voice. "Guess we're switching places."

The irony isn't lost on either of us. The timing is uncanny. With Damien jet-setting all over the world and Rafe in California, it didn't feel so hard to leave. But knowing Rafe will be back in my city again while I'm in another–across the ocean–is like one more punch to the gut.

"Well," I say slowly, "now I really don't know what to do."

"Do you have to make a decision today?" he asks gently.

"I have a little time." I glance toward the glowing laptop screen, the email still open. "But I feel like the second I choose, everything will change."

"Only if you let it," Rafe says. "No matter where you are, I'm still here. That doesn't change."

I chew the inside of my cheek. "You'd really be okay with me going to Paris for a year?"

"If it's what you want, then yes." He pauses. "But I'll definitely be counting the days until I can come visit and see you strutting around Paris like you own the place."

I laugh, the knot in my stomach loosening just a little. "I love you."

"I love you too, baby. So much."

When we hang up, I stare at my phone for a long time before turning back to my computer. The cursor blinks beside the word "accept." The offer is still there. It's the chance of a lifetime, but it's too complicated for me to decide right now.

I press the lid of the laptop closed and stand up, padding barefoot to the kitchen for a glass of water. I need to think. I need to talk to the others. I need to figure out if this is really what I want or just something I always thought I did.

There's only one way I know to work out the thoughts in my head. I grab my bag and keys and head out the door.

McKenzie is already at our studio when I arrive, hunched over one of her new pieces with a cup of cold brew in one hand and a paintbrush in the other. She's in her favorite paint-splattered overalls, her curls piled into a messy bun. Death metal blasts through the Bluetooth speakers. She says it calms her, but it gives me a migraine. I pick up her phone and press pause on her playlist.

"I didn't think you were stopping by today," she says without looking up.

"I just needed to come paint some things out of my system."

"Things like Paris?" she asks with a smirk

I nod, dropping my bag and setting up at my station. "I talked to Rafe about it."

Her eyes flick over to mine, wide with surprise. "What did he have to say?"

"He was so encouraging," I admit, doling out paints onto my palette. "You know how he is. He can't help but be complimentary."

"But?"

I sigh and pull on my apron. "He's coming back to Minnesota."

That gets her full attention. She sets her clay down carefully and turns to face me. "He what?"

"He just got traded back to the Vikings," I say with a nod, not taking my eyes off of my blank canvas for fear I might cry.

McKenzie whistles low. "Damn. That's bad timing."

"No kidding."

We work in silence for a while after that. Or at least, we try to. I get maybe three brushstrokes down before my mind buzzes again, and soon I'm just sitting there, staring at a half-formed abstract swirl of purple and gold, the Viking's colors, and thinking about everything I'd be leaving behind.

McKenzie finally breaks the silence. "Okay," she says, slamming a slab of clay on her pottery wheel and grabbing a wet paper towel to cover it. "We're doing this."

I raise an eyebrow. "What is it we're doing?"

"We're figuring out your life," she says, going over to one of the empty walls and pulling out a Sharpie.

"Should we really be writing on the wall?" I ask warily.

"You can just cover it with something fabulous later. But right now, we need a tried-and-true pros and cons list."

As she says this, she writes the words on the wall next to each other and underlines them neatly.

"Let's start with the pros," she instructs me.

I stare at her dumbfounded for a moment, realizing we're actually doing this, but I finally surrender to her particular brand of crazy.

"Well," I start. "It's Paris."

"Exactly," she says, writing it in large capital letters. "Besides the obvious one, how will moving to Paris help you?"

"It will be inspiring for my art. I have the opportunity to really grow in my career. It'll be a foot in the door of international art education, which could open up so many other experiences for me."

She nods as she writes all this quickly. "Keep going," she encourages me.

"There are endless galleries and cafés and art walks. I'll get to see what it feels like to be on my own in a place where no one knows me."

"That one sounds important for your personal growth," she murmurs, scribbling it with a little underline.

"And I think I just want to know I can do it. If I can go abroad for a year and succeed, what else will I be capable of?"

McKenzie finishes writing and looks over at me with a bright smile.

"I already know you're capable of incredible things," she says sweetly. "Now let's talk about cons."

I hesitate for a moment as I consider the only con that really matters to me. "I'll miss the guys."

"Fair," she says, writing that down in big letters to match the size of "PARIS" in the pro list. "That is definitely a con."

"I'll miss you," I continue.

"That's sweet but irrelevant. I would never expect you to give up something like this for me. Plus, we have FaceTime. What else?"

I shoot her a look, but she grins and keeps writing.

"Melody's due in two weeks," I say softly.

That wipes the smile right off her face. In fact, I see the effort it takes for her not to roll her eyes.

"Which really isn't your burden to bear," she says, putting a hand on her hip like she's ready to argue with me. "It's not a good reason to stay."

"She's already overwhelmed, and the baby isn't even here yet. What if she really needs me?"

McKenzie leans back, sighing.

"You threw her a baby shower. You've offered to help her in any way you can. But at the end of the day, you have your life and she has hers. She hasn't always been a great friend to you, and you know that if the tables were turned, she would go to Paris without a backward glance."

I don't say anything to that. Her words are harsh, but I know it's true. It's sad, knowing how close Melody and I used to be. I do want to help her, and to get to know her baby, but McKenzie is right.

"I guess the real con is leaving behind everything I've built here," I say finally. "I've started something big here, and if I leave for a year, everything might have to be on hold until I get back."

McKenzie considers this for a moment. "But it is just a year," she finally says. "A year isn't forever. Not even close. You wouldn't be starting from scratch, and you would have so many new experiences under your belt."

I nod slowly. "That's a good point."

She grabs my phone off my easel and opens the camera app, taking a picture of the wall. "Read that out loud to yourself. Then decide."

I take the phone, my eyes skimming over the list she's carefully written out. And as I read the words, I can see a life in Paris. I picture myself walking to class with a sketchpad under one arm, sitting on a balcony with a glass of wine, dancing in some dimly lit bar where no one cares who I am. I picture silence, space, and growth.

And then I picture Rafe in a Vikings jersey, running onto the field just twenty minutes from here. I picture Scott working the soil with his sleeves rolled up, and Tomás reading a poem aloud in Spanish just for me, and Damien ordering a private plane to fly me anywhere I want to go. I picture babysitting Melody's baby so she can have a much-needed night to herself.

My chest tightens. "I don't know what to do," I whisper.

McKenzie shrugs. "Then don't go for a full year. Ask them if you can just teach for a semester," she says simply. "Give yourself the chance to try it without the pressure of committing to the whole year. If you love it, stay. If you don't, come home. There's no rule that says you can't change your mind."

I blink at her. "That's actually brilliant."

"I know," she says smugly. "I'm full of wisdom. Like a hot, chaotic Yoda."

I laugh and walk over to hug her from behind, resting my chin on her shoulder. "Thank you."

"Don't thank me yet. You still have to tell the guys."

"Don't remind me," I groan.

She pats my arm. "You've already told Rafe. That's one down."

And three to go.

2

HOMECOMING

I immediately spot Harper through the wall of bodies at the baggage claim. Her hair is pulled back in that messy knot she always does when she's not trying too hard, and her smile is radiant. My chest goes warm immediately. I'm home.

Harper begins frantically waving the moment our eyes meet. She's wearing jeans and a navy hoodie that says "Minneapolis Art Girls" across the front in cracked white letters. I already know there are probably specks of paint all over it. I grab the strap of my carry-on tighter and weave through the crowd to get to my little artist.

"Hey, superstar," she teases as I get close, grinning up at me. "Catch any touchdowns lately?"

I lean in and kiss her before I say a word. Her mouth is soft and warm and familiar. She tastes like cinnamon gum and vanilla lip balm, a specific combination of hers that always makes me a little weak. I linger on her lips, giving her all the passion I've been saving up since she last visited.

"Hi," I say simply when we break apart.

She laughs breathlessly. "Hi."

I don't see the flash until after it happens, but the sound of a camera click is unmistakable. Then I hear another. I glance over my shoulder and see a guy with a DSLR pointed right at us. Another one joins him from the side, and I hear the murmuring begin.

"Is that—?" Harper begins before she's cut off.

"Rafe Maloney, how's it feel to be back in Minneapolis?" a paparazzo shouts to me.

"Rafe, who's your girlfriend?" asks another.

Click. Flash. Another burst of camera light.

Harper just arches a brow and leans against me, as nonchalant as if we were strolling through a Sunday farmer's market, and not as if we're currently being stalked by paparazzi at the baggage claim. I loop my arm around her waist and tug her closer.

"I didn't know I'd need sunglasses indoors," I groan. "Sorry you've gotten caught up in this."

"You're worth it," she answers with an amused smirk.

We walk to the exit. A few of the paparazzi follow for a bit, snapping more pictures of us holding hands and pretending to whisper to each other like we're scandalous. I lean down and murmur, "Should we make out in front of the vending machines to really sell it?"

"Only if you want your mom to call me," she says, laughing quietly.

"She'll probably start picking out baby names," I groan.

We keep walking, and they follow until we push through the exit doors and step into the crisp Minnesota air. It's colder here than it was in San Francisco, but it feels like home. I've missed the sharp, clean air and the way it clears my head. Thankfully, we lose the paparazzi by the time we get to the parking garage.

"Well," Harper says, tossing her keys in the air and catching them. "That wasn't as bad as I expected."

"Honestly, it could have been much worse," I admit sheepishly.

"I can't wait to see what sleazy headline they come up with," she laughs.

"'Vikings Star Player Seen Kissing Hot Artist,'" I joke, tossing my bag into the backseat of her car.

"More like, 'Who's The Slob With America's Hottest Football Star?'" she shoots back.

"I'm the slob," I say, looking down at my rumpled clothes. "And you are a sight for sore eyes."

I grab her hand and kiss it and she puts on a playlist of French indie pop. I tease her about how pretentious it sounds, but secretly I like it. She's clearly embracing the idea of this Paris job, and I couldn't be happier for her.

By the time we get to her place, I'm starving and running on nothing but fumes. As soon as we step in the door, I feel like I belong here. Even though I had my place before I left, Harper's apartment is much cozier and more lived in. Besides, being with her is much better than being alone.

"Sit," she commands. "I stocked the fridge with all your favorites. I can make you anything you want."

I stretch out on the couch and close my eyes. My body aches from the plane ride, and as much as I don't want to miss a moment with her, I can't help but give into the weariness. When I open my eyes again, Harper's standing over me with a meatball sub and a can of my favorite beer.

"You're spoiling me already," I say, sitting up.

"I've got to make up for lost time," she muses, kissing me chastely on the lips.

We eat on the couch, sharing bites and swapping stories.

"How do you feel about being back?"

I consider this as I chew on a meatball. "I'm excited," I say honestly. "Less excited that you're off soon, but I know you'll come back to me."

"I absolutely will," she says with a happy smile. "I talked to the school in Paris, and they've agreed to let me work for a semester and decide if I want to stay on for a whole year."

"That's amazing!" I beam.

A semester without Harper seems a lot easier to handle than an entire year. As much as I want to support her dreams, it's hard to let her go. I reach out and tuck a piece of her hair behind her ear.

"I'm really proud of you, baby."

Her eyes search mine. "Really? You aren't secretly plotting a way to keep me from going?"

"Of course not!" I can't help but laugh. "You are so talented, I would be a shit boyfriend to keep you here just because I'll miss you. You've always supported my dreams, and I'll do whatever you need to support yours."

She lets out a breath of relief and leans forward, her forehead pressing lightly to mine. "You have no idea how much that means to me," she breathes out.

"I think I do." I smile, kissing her gently.

* * *

HARPER

I let Rafe take a nap on my bed because he really does look exhausted. He'd never complain about it, but I know this move was a lot of work for him. He yawned in the middle of a kiss, and I knew it was time to force him to lie down. Once he was in bed, he was out in a minute. He didn't even take his shoes off.

I linger by the doorway, watching him for a little longer than is probably normal, then turn back to the living room.

I sit down, curling my legs underneath me, and pull a throw blanket over my lap, even though I'm not cold. It's more to comfort me, to hold me together while I consider these huge life plans in front of me.

I'm not remotely surprised that Rafe was so supportive. He's always been that way, even when he didn't understand something I was doing. In high school, he was always there to cheer me on at art shows and holding my hand at experimental galleries. Back then, it felt like he would hold my hand forever.

But today, I felt him give me the space to let go. Not of our relationship, of course, but more to let go of my worries. Even though he can't hold my hand through Paris, I know that I'm not going to lose him once I go. He'll always be there for me, waiting in the wings until I know what to do with the rest of my life.

It makes me want to cry a little, honestly. There's something about being loved that way, so fully and without conditions, that feels overwhelming. Because it sets the bar high. It makes me wonder how the others will take the news. I haven't told Scott, Tomas, or Damien, and I don't know that they'll have the same reaction.

Even though I know they love me, even though I trust them, it's still hard to predict how they'll respond to the news that I'm leaving, even though it's only temporary.

Scott, I think, will understand. He's grounded and level-headed enough to understand that this decision doesn't take anything away from him. He might not like it, but he won't show it. He'll smile for me all the way to the departure gate.

Damien is a little trickier, but only because he's going to want to take care of everything. He'll book flights, rent penthouses, try to build me an art studio in the middle of the Left Bank before I even finish telling him about the opportunity. And I don't want any of it. This is my chance to prove myself on my own, and that's what I'm most worried about.

My sweet, passionate Tomas is going to be thrilled. I know that. But I'm also most nervous about telling him. I don't want him to worry about what it means. He may think that I'm pulling away or trying to chase something he can't give me. He's so deeply rooted in his life, so well-established, and I don't want him to think this is about needing something more. I only hope I can make him see how much he means to me, even though I'm leaving the country for a while.

My phone buzzes on the arm of the couch. I reach for it instinctively, already dreading the possibility that it's my mom. The paparazzi photos from the airport have been floating around online for hours now, and while it's mostly harmless, just fluffy headlines like "Quarterback Rafe Maloney Spotted with Mystery Woman," I know how quickly the narrative can shift. All it takes is one person recognizing me, one thread connecting the dots from Rafe to

Damien, and then I'll have paparazzi following my every move for weeks.

Thank God it was Rafe I was seen kissing, because my parents at least know him and they won't think it's a huge deal. My mom will probably be thrilled. Maybe. Possibly.

I'm not ready for them to know that I'm dating Rafe and Tomas and Scott and Damien. I don't want them to know that I love four men and that none of them is a side fling or a temporary indulgence. They would absolutely lose their shit and probably cut me out of their lives forever.

They can't possibly understand that I love who I love, and it's not in the perfect, cookie-cutter way that they would want for me. It's a lot more complicated than that.

The photos will probably hit some of the smaller sites. Maybe a tabloid or two. I can't imagine it's going to be on any national gossip site. Rafe is popular, but he's no Travis Kelce. I'd be surprised if it even reaches one of the gossip sites my mom pretends not to read.

I take a breath and tell myself that I'm probably safe for now. And once I'm in Paris, I won't have to worry about what my parents think. There will be an entire ocean between us, and if they want to call me a "whore" or an "unscrupulous woman," they'll have to do it over the phone. And I know that will be much less satisfying than saying it to my face.

3

———

DIFFICULT NEWS

Harper's on edge today, and I can't figure out why. It's just there in the subtle shift in her energy and the way her smile doesn't quite reach her eyes. She seems distracted, and even a little distant. There's definitely something on her mind, and she isn't letting me in. That isn't like her, and it has me worried.

"You look beautiful," I murmur as I finish clasping the necklace she chose for the baby shower. It's a delicate gold thing with a tiny opal pendant that rests just below her collarbone. My clumsy fingers could hardly work the clasp, but she asked me to help anyway. She was too jittery to do it herself.

"Thank you," she says, her voice light but somehow off.

I watch her in the mirror, unsure whether to press it or to leave it alone. She smooths her dress over her hips, then adjusts the sleeves. She's fidgety, picking and pulling like she can't make it fit just right.

The shower is all set up, and our dinner reservation isn't for another hour, but she's been ready for the last twenty minutes. It's unusual behavior for her, considering she's usually late to everything. She likes to make an entrance.

"You sure you're okay?" I ask, resting my hands on her shoulders. Her skin is warm beneath the fabric of her dress. "You've been quiet today."

She meets my eyes in the mirror and offers a quick, vacant smile. "I just have a lot on my mind," she shrugs nonchalantly.

I nod, letting her have the space. But a thread of worry begins weaving through my thoughts anyway.

As we head out, I open the car door for her, and she gives me a grateful nod, brushing her hair behind her ear. She's always more graceful than she realizes, even when she's not trying to be. Especially then. But I can't enjoy the drive because she's still quiet, looking out the window instead of at me, twisting the strap of her bag around her fingers.

By the time I pull onto the parkway, I can't take it anymore. "Did I do something wrong, mi amor?" I blurt out, lacking her grace.

She turns to look at me, startled. "What do you mean? Of course you haven't!" she assures me, grabbing my hand and squeezing gently.

"You're not yourself today," I tell her directly. "You're quiet and picky, and I'm losing my mind. Mierda! If you want to end things, just let me know now so we can get it over with."

She sighs, sinking a little deeper into her seat, and my heart breaks a little.

This is it; I know it.

"I'm sorry," she whispers quietly, and I hold my breath. "I don't mean to be weird. I've just got something to tell you, and I'm nervous."

"Nervous?" I repeat, gripping the steering wheel a little tighter. It's all I can do not to break it in two. "Are you nervous about us?"

"Of course not!" she immediately answers, running her hand through my hair in a comforting gesture. "But I have something to tell you, and I'm not sure how you're going to take it."

That doesn't help. At all.

"Okay," I say quietly. "Now I'm terrified."

She lets out a laugh, soft and rueful. "Don't be. I promise it's not what you think."

I glance at her as we approach a red light. She's chewing on her lip now, another sign that something big is coming. I feel it coiling in my chest, the awful thought that she's about to pull away.

"Can you just tell me," I ask gently, "before I work myself into some worst-case scenario?"

She hesitates, watching the road ahead, then says, "Okay. But not while you're driving."

We ride in silence for another few minutes before the restaurant comes into view. I pull into the lot, my heart hammering like I just ran a mile uphill. When I park, I shift into neutral and turn to face her, bracing myself.

She takes a deep breath, then looks at me. "I got offered a teaching position in Paris."

For a moment, all I can do is blink at her. It's not at all what I expected to hear. My mind doubles back as I think through all the horrific scenarios I'd imagined, and none of them make sense with what she's just said.

I exhale slowly, trying to catch up. "Harper, that's incredible!" I finally manage as the tension in my chest eases and transforms into pride.

"You're not mad?"

"Mad?" I let out a short, breathy laugh. "Mi amor, I thought you were about to tell me you didn't want to see me anymore. But this is terrific! Of course, you should teach art in Paris!"

She lets her head fall back against the seat, laughing with something like relief. "God, no. No, Tomás. I could never—"

"I was scared," I admit. "You've not been yourself, and I thought I'd done something wrong."

She reaches for my hand, curling her fingers through mine. "You are absolutely perfect, and that's what made it so hard to tell you," she says quietly. "I just didn't know how you'd take it. You have a life here. You're established. I didn't want you to think this is me trying to pull away from you."

I shake my head, lifting her hand to my lips. "As a fellow educator, I could never begrudge you such an amazing opportunity," I tell her seriously. "And as a man who loves you, I would be a huge burro if I weren't thrilled for you."

"I'm only going for one semester," she adds quickly. "If I love it, I'll stay. If not, I'll come home."

"Selfishly, I hope you hate it," I joke, brushing my thumb over her knuckles. "But I'm so proud of you. Unbelievably proud. You deserve this."

"You think so?" she asks, her brow creasing again with nervousness.

"I think you are the most incredible woman in the world," I tell her honestly.

She exhales, and something in her posture loosens. Then, with a sudden shift in the air between us, she leans in, close enough that I can feel her breath on my face.

When she kisses me, it's slow at first, like a thank-you, or just relief. But then her hands twist into my hair and her tongue darts into my mouth. Hunger threads through the kiss until we're leaning toward each other across the center console, her fingers tugging at the collar of my shirt, my hand sliding up the back of her neck. We are devouring each other.

I pull back just enough to murmur, "Are you hungry? Because I don't think I can go into that restaurant and not try to tear your clothes off."

She's breathless.

"I'm starving," she says earnestly, but then her mouth turns up in a smirk. "But food is the last thing on my mind."

I break away from her reluctantly and reach for the ignition, turning the key with a snap.

"Good," I say. "Because I'm taking you home."

* * *

Harper

The second Tomás turns onto his street, I'm already leaning across the center console, one hand curled behind his neck, my lips brushing the edge of his jawline. I can feel the tightness in his shoulders as he tries to keep his eyes on the road, but I don't make it easy. My other hand is resting on his thigh, just above his knee, my fingers splayed out to drive him wild. I don't want him to crash, but I do want him to be ready the moment we're inside.

"You keep doing that," he murmurs, his voice low, a little strained, "and we're not making it inside."

I smile against his skin. "Then drive faster!" I almost whine.

"I'm going thirty-five in a thirty," he says, shifting his grip on the wheel.

"Would you rather be pulled over for speeding or arrested for public indecency, because that's where this is headed," I tease.

He exhales a laugh, but there's tension beneath it. I'm not the only one buzzing with this desire. I squeeze my thighs together, so ready for him it hurts.

I'm so relieved by how well he took the Paris news, and now all I want is to show him how grateful I am. More than grateful, I want him. I need him. My body and my heart are perfectly aligned on that. I want to show him exactly how little distance I want between us.

When he pulls into the driveway, I'm already unbuckling my seatbelt. The moment the engine cuts off, I'm out the door, nearly sprinting to his front door. He isn't far behind me, and soon he has me pinned against the solid frame, his teeth scraping against my neck.

"Inside," I say, my breath catching. "Now."

He doesn't hesitate. He unlocks the door with one hand while his other arm wraps around my waist, holding me close. We stumble into the house together, breathless and clumsy with urgency. As soon as the door clicks shut behind us, I'm pressing him back against it, my fingers already threading into his hair, pulling his mouth to mine.

The kiss is hungry, open, and messy. There's nothing slow or sweet about it. I bite his bottom lip, and he groans, gripping my hips to show me exactly how much he likes that.

"Bedroom?" I whisper, tugging at the hem of his shirt and pulling me back.

"I won't make it that far, Corazón," he mutters against my mouth.

"Then take me right here," I growl hungrily.

His hands move to the hem of my dress, pulling it over my head in a quick, dizzying movement. I kiss his neck as I take off his belt, electrified by the sound of the buckle hitting the floor. His chest heaves as I run my hands down it, scraping my fingernails gently over his hard muscles.

His eyes roam over me slowly, reverently, and the heat in his gaze makes me flush all over.

"Beautiful," he says, so softly it nearly breaks me.

But his movements are anything but soft as he spins me around and pins me to the door, pulling up my leg to wrap around his waist. He is rock hard and impatient, and I know he can feel my heat, the way the liquid pools in my panties.

We'll have time for slow and sweet later. Right now, we are just desperate beings who can't survive without the other.

He trails kisses down my neck, my collarbone, my chest. His hands slide over my waist, my thighs, memorizing every curve, squeezing and groping and causing me to lose my breath. I arch my back against the door, rubbing myself against his length, and he curses in Spanish.

"Fuck me hard against your door," I tell him seductively. "Then take me to your bedroom and show me just how nervous you were earlier."

"You're la diabla," he laughs, but he slips out of his boxers and quickly pulls down my panties.

Then he lifts me up by my ass and enters me as I wrap my legs around him. I nearly collapse against the door, and would definitely fall if he weren't holding me up. I am so wet and ready for him; the instant contact is both delicious and not enough.

"You feel like home, mi amor," he gasps as he drills into me. "You are mi hogar."

I grasp the back of his head, holding on for dear life as he goes deeper and deeper inside, like he's trying to bury himself there. Part of me wants him to, for him to carve out a space that is just his, that no one else can ever touch.

I feel the pressure start to build, and my body tenses around him. I am so unbelievably close to the edge as he whispers more sweet and downright filthy things in my ear. He tells me he loves me. He tells me he wants to fuck me on top of the Eiffel Tower for all of Paris to see. He tells me he's proud of me. He tells me he's going to leave a mark so I don't forget him.

What he doesn't know is he's already marked me. It's not anything he can see or touch, but there's a space in my heart that has his name written in big, bold letters. And it's his name I scream out so loud, I'm sure the neighbors are going to complain. It's his name I whisper as I cover his chest, his neck, and his face in soft, sweet kisses.

It's his name I'll be moaning again and again when he takes me back to his bedroom and takes his time with me.

4

———

FLEUR DE LIS

The baby shower is basically perfect, if I do say so myself. Tomas and I did an amazing job transforming the art studio into an explosion of pastel pinks and blues. Melody decided to wait until the birth to find out the sex of the baby, so we made sure to balance both.

Melody, despite being eight months pregnant and visibly exhausted, is glowing. Her cheeks are flushed as she smiles at the many people who've come to wish her well... the same people who make sure to tell me how everything looks.

I can't help but beam and text Tomas to thank him for helping me string pastel garlands and assemble handmade paper flowers to decorate the long buffet table. Damien came through with a contact who would do the food as a personal favor. There's a ridiculous tower of tiny sandwiches, platters of charcuterie arranged in the shape of a heart, and even a mimosa bar, though Melody's glass is filled with sparkling apple cider and garnished with three strawberries and a paper umbrella.

It should be a perfect day, but I've been holding my breath since the moment I spotted my parents walking through the door. They weren't even supposed to come. When I invited them, it was more of a gesture than anything. I figured they'd at least send Mel a gift and leave it at that.

Yet there they are, my mother in a long floral skirt and fitted blazer, her hair swept into the same no-nonsense bun she's worn since I was in middle school. My father, buttoned up to the throat, grips a wrapped gift in both hands like he's holding a bomb.

They've already said hello to Melody and offered a few polite smiles to the guests. My dad complimented the meatballs. My mom asked if the napkins could have been a slightly more modest shade of pink. They're stalling, and we all know it.

Halfway through the gift opening, while Melody is holding up a tiny onesie that says "Born to Sparkle," my mom touches my arm and asks if she can speak to me privately. Her voice is soft, but her eyes are sharp, and my chest instinctually tightens.

I step away with her toward the hallway near the supply closet. My dad follows a beat later, his hands clasped behind his back like he's bracing for battle. I already know this is about those damn paparazzi pictures.

"I wanted to ask you something," my mom begins, folding her hands. "I thought it would be better to address it privately."

"And it couldn't wait until after the party?" I ask, feeling annoyed.

It's rude to be doing this in the middle of everything, but she already thinks Melody has ruined her life. It's nothing to my mother to disappear during the gift opening.

"Melody showed me something on her phone earlier," she says. "A picture of you at the airport. With Rafael."

I plaster on a polite expression, the one I save for family functions and religious holidays, but it takes all my energy not to roll my eyes at her.

"Oh?" I pretend to be surprised.

"You were kissing him," she adds, as if I might not know.

My father clears his throat, shifting uncomfortably beside her.

"In public," he adds, his voice low, "with photographers present."

My mother's eyes narrow, but she doesn't raise her voice. She never does. It's worse that way. "We just want to understand why you would allow yourself to be photographed in such an unladylike light."

There's a beat of silence, broken only by the distant sound of Melody laughing as she opens another gift.

"I wasn't aware I was being photographed," I say evenly. "And I don't think kissing someone I'm in a relationship with is 'unladylike.'"

My mother's lips press together. "It's about appearances, Harper."

"Which you've made clear my whole life," I mutter before I can stop myself.

She stiffens. "It's unbecoming to put yourself on display like that. What will people think? What kind of message are you sending?"

I let out a breath and lean back against the wall. "That I'm in love with someone and not ashamed of it?"

My dad shifts uncomfortably again, like the he's hoping the floor might open up beneath us. "We know you and Rafael dated in high school. And he's familiar to the family. But Harper, you're not a teenager anymore."

"Exactly," I say. "I'm an adult. I get to decide who I kiss, when I kiss them, and where I kiss them."

I can feel my heartbeat speeding up, that all-too-familiar mix of anger and hurt climbing up the back of my throat. I want to scream. I want to cry. I want to tell them it could have been worse. That it could've been a picture of me with Damien, Tomás, or Scott. That they should be grateful it was Rafe. At least he fits their mold of the successful, charming, all-American athlete.

Instead, I take a steadying breath and look them both in the eyes.

"I'm not embarrassed," I say. "And I'm not interested in hiding my happiness to make anyone more comfortable, not even you."

It's quiet for a long moment.

Then my mother smooths the front of her skirt, her eyes flicking toward the party room. "Well," she huffs. "It's clear to us that you don't care what we think about this, so we won't mention it again. But, really Harper, think about how it makes us look."

"Trust me, Mom." I laugh humorlessly. "When I'm with the man I love, I'm not thinking of you at all."

I want so badly to say "men I love," but I don't want to start a fight in the middle of the party.

She gives me a look I know too well. It's equal parts exasperation and disappointment.

"Please give Melody our apologies," she says with a watery expression. "I'm suddenly not feeling very well."

She turns toward the door and leaves, with my father towing behind in an awkward shuffle. He's probably upset they're leaving before we cut the cake.

I stay in the hallway for a minute, just long enough to unclench my fists and breathe. When I walk back into the room, McKenzie catches my eye instantly. She raises one brow in a silent question. I shake my head slightly, offering a thin smile. *Later,* I mouth. She nods.

Melody is still holding court in the center of the room, surrounded by tissue paper and baby socks and enough pink tulle to smother a small village. She looks happy. Radiant. She deserves that.

And so do I.

Still, as I grab a mimosa and pretend to be fascinated by the baby monitor she just unwrapped, I can't help the ache in my chest. Even though I don't want to care what my parents think, some part of me still does, and I hate that.

The rest of the shower blurs by in a haze of smiling and posing for pictures and making small talk with people I only sort of know. Melody pulls me in for a hug before she leaves, her belly pressing into mine as she thanks me again and again for everything.

Once she's gone, I help McKenzie clean up, the two of us working in silence until the floor is no longer coated in glitter and cake crumbs.

"You okay?" she asks finally, handing me a garbage bag.

"Yeah," I lie. "Fine."

She gives me a knowing look that cuts to the quick.

"Hey," I say softly, changing the subject, "thanks for sticking around today. For everything."

She shrugs. "What are best friends for?" she grins.

"I still can't believe Melody showed them that photo."

"She probably didn't mean to," she says genuinely. "I mean, I know she's been a toxic bitch in the past, but I really think she didn't mean to be hurtful this time. I noticed today that she's a little ditzy. Is that pregnancy brain, or is she always like that?"

"Definitely pregnancy brain," I laugh. "She's usually very put together and organized."

"Well, then let's chalk it all up to the hormones and assume it wasn't a slap in the face after you organized this gorgeous party for her," she finally says as she closes off a bag of trash. "And now that the party is officially over, let's talk about something more important. Like, have you told everyone about the move yet?"

"Two down," I laugh. "I haven't seen Damien in a while. I think he's been in Brussels or something. And Scott and I have a date planned in a few days, so I figured I'd tell him then."

"They'll both be as thrilled as Rafe was," she assures me. "How did Tomas take it?"

I can't help but blush as I think about just how well he took it. And how well I took him later on. "He was happy for me," I say carefully.

"He must have been really happy if you're that red," she laughs. "What even is your life?"

I laugh, turning toward the front door as I hear the faint clunk of footsteps outside. The studio is technically closed now, and we locked up half an hour ago. I glance at McKenzie.

"Are you expecting someone?"

"Nope," she says, her eyes narrowed. "Unless the stork's coming early."

A firm knock echoes through the door. I walk over cautiously, peeking through the window, and back up in surprise when I see a guy in a green apron holding a bouquet of flowers.

"Delivery," he calls through the glass.

I open the door and smile politely. "Hi," I say, a little flustered. "If these are for the baby shower, you're a little late."

"These are for–" He stops and looks at his tablet. "Harper Ward."

"That's me," I say, surprised.

He hands me the bouquet with a little bow wrapped around the stems, and I can't help but stare at how gorgeous they are.

"Enjoy your evening," he says before disappearing down the hallway.

I stare at the irises. They're gorgeous, a deep violet and blue. I bring them inside as I hold them to my nose, the scent faint but unmistakably elegant. McKenzie's already leaning in, her eyes gleaming with curiosity.

"Oooh. Someone's got a secret admirer."

"Doubtful," I mutter, fingers skimming over the crisp edges of the card nestled inside.

I pull it out and read aloud:

"Congratulations to my fleur-de-lis."

McKenzie gasps. "Oh, come on. That's sexy and pretentious. It has to be Damien. He must be back from 'Brussels or something,'" she teases.

I bite my lip, but the smile's already forming. Before I can respond, my phone buzzes in my pocket. Naturally, it's Damien.

I answer with a smirk. "You have impeccable timing."

His voice hums through the speaker, smooth as melted chocolate.

"You must have just gotten the flowers."

"I did," I confirm. "You sent me irises."

"I did," he answers confidently, and I can hear the chuckle in his voice.

"Iris is the flower of France," I add pointedly.

"You're far too clever for your own good, mon amour."

McKenzie makes a swooning motion in the background and collapses onto the couch dramatically. I flick a crumpled napkin at her and turn away, lowering my voice.

"Thank you. They're beautiful."

"I wanted you to feel celebrated," he says. "I heard from a little bird that you've officially accepted the Paris offer."

"Only for one semester," I clarify, even though I know he already knows.

"It's still worth celebrating. My little red bird is taking flight."

My heart warms at that. "Speaking of birds, was the one who told you about Paris named Rafe, by chance?"

"Perhaps," he says smoothly. "Or perhaps I simply have eyes and ears everywhere."

"That's a little creepy."

"You think it's sexy, don't you?" he says gruffly, and the sound shoots straight to my core.

"Have dinner with me."

My smile grows. "Tonight?"

"Yes," he nearly growls. "I've missed you."

I glance at McKenzie, who gives me a thumbs-up without even hearing the question.

"I'd love to," I say.

"I'll pick you up in an hour."

5

———

MIDDLE OF THE NIGHT CALL

Harper's waiting outside the studio when I pull up. The light from the streetlamp halos her hair, making her look like a goddamn angel. Her arms are bare despite the evening chill, and she's tucking a strand of strawberry-blonde behind her ear in a delicate, almost unconscious motion that drives me wild.

I step out of the car before the driver can get to it and round the front.

"You'll spoil me," she says as I open the door for her.

I lean in slightly, just close enough to breathe her in. "Darling, I intend to."

She laughs, and I don't miss the blush that sprinkles her cheeks.

Inside the car, she settles beside me, tucking her legs to the side and nuzzling against me. Her fingers rest lightly on the edge of her clutch, and when she glances at me, her eyes are full of warmth.

"The flowers were beautiful," she says softly. "Thank you."

"I thought about sending you a pair of Cartier earrings, but the irises seemed more appropriate."

Her lips curve. "Because I hate jewelry?" she jokes, almost looking a little disappointed.

"Because you're not a woman easily impressed by flashy things. Any schmuck could send you diamond earrings, but only a man who knows you would choose a flower that symbolizes your forthcoming journey."

She rolls her eyes, but her smile deepens. "You really don't miss anything."

"I don't make a habit of missing what matters," I say, and I mean it.

There's a moment of stillness. Then she turns her head and looks at me more seriously.

"How do you do that?" she asks. "You always know what I need before I do."

I shrug, adjusting the cuff of my shirt. "I am deeply obsessed with you," I tease. "And I listen when you talk."

"But I hadn't told you about Paris yet. So what is it, a crystal ball? A hidden camera? Who are these 'little birdies' that, apparently, aren't Rafe?"

I can't help but chuckle at her curiosity. "Let's just say that I make sure that I'm alerted about any news about you," I say cryptically.

"You could always just wait for me to tell you things," she says through slitted eyes.

"But, little red bird, where is the fun in that?" I don't miss the way her body trembles in excitement from my words.

The car slows in front of one of our favorite restaurants. The maître d' opens the door the moment he sees us, and I take Harper's hand as she steps out, guiding her inside.

Our table is tucked into a private corner, candlelight flickering between us. The wine appears without the need to request it, and Harper eyes the deep red liquid with suspicion.

"Mr. Blackwood," she says in a haughty tone. "Are you planning on getting me drunk?"

"I never plan for your intoxication," I say, grinning. "It's just a delightful consequence."

We sip and settle, the easy rhythm of us finding its natural pace.

When the wine starts to relax her, she tells me about a disastrous run-in with her parents.

"They were scandalized," she says, cutting into her dinner. "You'd think I'd been caught doing something actually indecent."

"They're lucky it was Rafe and not me," I murmur, sipping my wine.

She glances up. "Why is that?"

"I wouldn't have stopped at just kissing you."

She nearly chokes on her food. "Damien!"

"I'm just being honest," I say, my voice low. "In fact, it's hard for me to keep my hands off you right now."

"You're going to cause a national scandal," she giggles.

I reach across the table and brush my thumb along the back of her hand. "I have enough money to make sure it never reaches the press," I murmur.

Her breath catches, just slightly, and I let the moment hang there before I release her and lean back again.

We talk through the main course, through dessert, and through another glass of wine she insists she hates but keeps sipping. When the plates are cleared and the candles have burned halfway down, I finally shift the conversation toward the thing I've been waiting to discuss.

"So," I say. "Paris. You haven't told me how you feel about going."

She stiffens, just slightly. "I have some complicated feelings," she admits shyly. "I mean, of course I'm excited. It's Paris!"

She emphasizes the words with so much awe that I have to remind myself that she's never been there. A place that's become almost boring to me is a place of wonder to her, and I want the chance to experience it through her eyes.

"But," I prod, knowing there's more.

"But," she continues, "leaving is hard. And I'm nervous. It's a new city, and as much as I have the chance to grow into myself, I could also make a complete idiot of myself."

"You could never make an idiot of yourself," I assure her. "I bet half the male population will be enamored with you the moment you step off the plane."

"Yes, that's what I need," she laughs. "More men to juggle."

"Then let me come with you. I'll fly you there and stay with you the first week. I'll help you get settled and then leave you alone to show them what a star you are."

Her eyes widen. "Damien—"

"Sorry, that wasn't a suggestion," I tell her with a smirk. "I'm coming with you."

"You're serious."

"I'll find a penthouse nearby. I won't be underfoot. I'll take you to every café and gallery and artist's studio you've ever dreamed about, and then I'll leave you to your work. But I won't let you land there alone."

Emotion flickers across her face, surprise first, then relief. Then something I don't quite recognize. Vulnerability, maybe.

"You really do think of everything," she whispers.

"I think of you."

We sit in silence for a moment, the city outside the window breathing softly around us.

Then she reaches for my hand, and I close my fingers around hers.

* * *

Harper

It's impossible not to fall a little harder for Damien every time we're together. He may be a bit of a stalker, but he's also unbelievably thoughtful. Knowing he'll be in Paris with me for a week helps calm some of my nerves about the trip.

On our way back to his penthouse, he tells me stories about Paris. He's been there so many times, he's practically a native. I can't wait to see his version of Paris, the art scene and the cafés that only the locals know about.

In the car, we touch each other as inconspicuously as possible, but

I'm itching to get my hands on him. Everything about this impromptu date has been perfect, and my body is so desperate for him. It's been weeks, and he knows how to get me going in a way that is so uniquely him.

When we finally reach his penthouse, he places his hand on my lower back and guides me inside, like his hand is magnetically drawn there. When we get inside, he turns to me with a look that tells me we aren't going to be sleeping much tonight.

"You're dangerous," I murmur as he steps closer.

"So are you," he replies, brushing a strand of hair from my face.

I smile, but it fades when his fingers slide along my jaw. His gaze drops to my mouth, and I can feel the shift in the room, in the air, in my blood. Then he kisses me.

It starts slowly, teasing, his lips barely brushing mine. But it deepens quickly. He kisses like a man who knows what he wants, and he has the self-control to take his time getting it. His hands slide over my waist, my hips, then down to the backs of my thighs as he lifts me effortlessly. I wrap my legs around him without thinking, a soft gasp escaping as he carries me across the room.

He lays me down gently on the edge of his massive bed, pausing only to tug his shirt over his head. My breath catches in my throat at the sight of him, the way it always does. He's so chiseled, he might have been carved by Michelangelo.

"I'm going to take my time with you, little red bird," he hums. "I'm going to show you exactly how much I've missed you, and exactly how much I'm going to lavish you in Paris. Consider this an apéritif."

"I like it when you talk dirty to me," I say with a light laugh, though inside I feel like I'm about to collapse. I just know he's about to devastate me in the best way possible.

His grin is wicked. "Je vais te baiser si fort que tu verras Dieu," he says in an accent so sexy it makes my knees go weak.

"My French is a little rusty," I admit breathlessly. "I heard something about God, I think."

"Trust me," he murmurs. "You'll understand perfectly when I'm done with you, little red bird."

"I can't wait," I groan.

He slides my dress up slowly, his fingers tracing every inch of newly exposed skin. I shiver beneath his touch, every nerve in my body alive and wanting. His lips follow his fingers, and when his kisses meet my inner thigh, I swear I forget how to breathe.

He worships me with his mouth, lighting my body up like a wildfire. Whether he kisses my skin for five minutes or five hours, I'm not sure. I'm transformed into pure, unadulterated need. Nothing exists in this world except for him and his lips on my collarbone, in the spot below my taught nipple, just a breath away from my clit. I'm begging him to sink into me, to put me out of my misery and make me fall apart.

"Not yet," he growls. "Not 'til I've had my fill."

Then he's between my legs, devouring me so thoroughly, I feel his tongue on every nerve. He laps me up, making my body quiver with each flick of his tongue. Then he carefully slips two fingers in me, curling them deep inside. I nearly radiate off the bed as my pleasure consumes me.

But there's no time to focus on that pleasure, because the moment I hit my peak, he positions himself right at my entrance and thrusts in hard and fast. He fucks me through my orgasm, and unbelievably, I feel the pleasure building even higher when I'm finished.

It's unlike anything I've ever experienced before. I'm flying to heights I didn't know were even possible. He's thrusting wildly, pulling my legs around him and grasping my ass as he pounds into me with reckless abandon.

"Yes!" I scream, not caring if the whole city hears. "So damn good."

"You're mine," he growls, and I nearly come apart right then. "Tell me you're mine."

"I'm yours," I moan so loud it makes my throat ache.

I cling to him, gasping as wave after wave builds inside me. His hands are everywhere, on my waist, in my hair, cupping my cheek as he kisses me again. And when I come apart beneath him again, I feel like I'm on another planet. He follows seconds later, burying his face against my neck as he shudders and collapses beside me.

Finally, after we've both returned to Earth, he turns to me with a satisfied smirk.

"So, little red bird, did you see God?"

I can't help but laugh as his earlier words in French make sense.

"I think I did," I breathe, curling into him.

* * *

It's the middle of the night when my phone rings. I wake groggy and confused, the sheet tangled around my waist and Damien's arm heavy across my stomach. I reach for the phone on the nightstand and squint at the screen. It's Melody.

That can only mean one thing at this hour. I sit up instantly and answer the call.

"Harper," Melody says, her voice breathless and high. "I think it's time."

I'm already out of bed, grabbing my clothes from the floor. "Is someone with you?"

"No." She stops abruptly, and I imagine her wincing in unimaginable pain. "I didn't want to wake anyone, but my water broke. Harp, I'm scared."

"Okay," I say, as calmly as I can. "I'm coming to get you. Stay put. I'm on my way."

Damien is already out of bed, pulling on his pants. "What happened?"

"Melody's in labor," I tell him, feeling the color drain from my face.

Ten minutes later, Damien's driver is pulling up in front of Melody's building, and I'm sprinting across the sidewalk barefoot, my heels clutched in one hand. Melody meets me at the door in a hoodie and pajama shorts, with one hand pressed to her lower back and the other braced against the doorframe.

"Hey," I say softly, wrapping an arm around her. "I've got you."

She nods, but her eyes are wide and scared. "I didn't think it would hurt this early."

I help her down the stairs, my heart pounding. Damien opens the back door and guides us in, his expression sharp and focused.

"It'll be alright," he says quietly. "Let's get you to the hospital."

Melody groans through another contraction, gripping my hand hard.

"Okay," I whisper, brushing her hair from her face. "Deep breaths. You're not alone."

She stops for just a second, grabbing my arm and looking at me with so much pain in her eyes.

"You'll never know what this means to me," she whispers, before another contraction hits her and she nearly doubles over in pain.

6

MAY

It's just past three A.M. when Melody's baby girl finally comes into the world. It's sort of a terrifying event. I hold Melody's hand as she screams her lungs out and cries that she can't take any more pain. For some stupid reason, she'd decided she was too strong for pain meds.

I do what I can to help. I hold her hand and wipe her head and tell her everything is going to be okay, even though I don't know if that's remotely true. But when her daughter comes into the world, screaming almost as loud as Melody, I am in awe.

She's absolutely beautiful.

She's all red and scrunched up and still covered in goopy stuff, but she's breathtakingly beautiful. Her lungs are strong, pushing out her cries for the whole world to hear. Already, she's showing that she's a force to be reckoned with, just like her mother.

In the silence that follows, a strange peace descends on all of us. I feel a lump rise in my throat as I watch Melody cradle her daughter for the first time. She's trembling, her hands unsure, her eyes glassy with awe and possibly fear.

"You did it, Mama," I whisper.

Melody nods, swallowing hard. "Yeah. I did. And she's perfect."

The baby calms a little in her arms. I watch them together, mother and daughter, and I can't help but wonder whether Melody is up to this challenge. It's not up to me to make that call, of course, but the baby is clearly strong-willed. She came three weeks early, after all.

The nurses begin moving around again, doing the necessary post-birth things, murmuring something about getting the baby into the neonatal unit, and I step aside to give them space.

Melody barely looks up. She's still staring at her baby like she's not entirely convinced she's real. Neither am I, for that matter.

* * *

MELODY ENDS UP HAVING TO STAY IN THE HOSPITAL FOR A WHILE. THE baby, who she's affectionately decided to call "May" for the month she was born, spent time in the neonatal intensive care unit since she was premature, though the doctors were impressed with her quick progress.

Melody was discharged with no problems, but she refuses to leave the hospital, staying at May's side, and I don't blame her. I spend the next few weeks practically living there along with her.

When May is finally cleared to be discharged, I'm still there, and I'm glad to bring them home.

The first thing I notice when I walk through Melody's door, car seat in hand, is that it looks like a Pinterest board threw up. Some of the decorations from the baby shower are in a heap in the corner, likely meant to be hung up before baby May arrived, but unfortunately Melody didn't have any time.

The entryway and living room are absolutely stacked with boxes of baby things, from diapers to a playpen. There's a bassinet set up in one corner of the small dining room, and I notice the kitchen table is littered with unopened mail, as well as a few bottles and an unopened pacifier.

Melody shuffles inside wearing oversized sweatpants and a hoodie that she stole from me in high school. She carries May, who's swaddled in a soft pink blanket McKenzy bought for her. In comparison, I feel like a pack mule. In addition to the car seat, I also have a diaper bag and May's discharge paperwork.

Melody carefully sets May down in the basinet before she sinks into the couch and curls up into herself. She looks tiny and terrified, and I don't even know how to help her.

"Do you want me to make some tea?" I ask, setting the bags down.

"Sure," she says, her voice barely above a whisper.

She's quieter than I've ever seen her, and her body looks heavy with exhaustion. But what scares me the most is how fragile she seems. I'm worried she's just seconds from falling apart, and I'm the only one around to put her back together.

I busy myself in the kitchen, filling the kettle, finding her only tea, searching for two clean mugs. It takes longer than it should because her kitchen is just as messy as her living area. I give the mugs a good rinse, just in case. I watch her from the doorway as the water boils. May hasn't stirred, thankfully, but neither has Melody. Her eyes are open, but she's staring into nothing.

"Do you want sugar in your tea?" I ask, trying to keep my voice casual.

She nods. "Yeah. Thanks."

I pour the tea, adding a generous amount of sugar to hers, and bring her a cup. I sit down beside her, but she doesn't move. We sit in silence for a while. She just lays there, curled in a ball and clutching her mug.

"She's perfect," I say softly, looking over to the basinet.

Melody smiles faintly. "She is."

"You've done so well, Mel. Really."

She gives a little shrug. "She cries a lot," she says blankly.

"She's a baby." I laugh lightly, hoping to break the tension. "That's sort of her job."

"I didn't think it would be this hard," she whispers.

"Everyone feels that way," I assure her, though truthfully, I have no idea. Melody is the first person I know to have a baby.

She doesn't respond, and the silence that falls between us feels tense.

I glance around the room again, really taking it all in. There's so much to do. There are stacks of unopened furniture boxes that are full of items that still need to be put together. I shudder to think what the nursery looks like. I wonder if any of it is ready, but I don't think asking her is going to make her feel better.

Eventually, Melody falls asleep, the tea still in her hands. I carefully take it away from her and place it on the coffee table, trying not to disturb her. I grab my phone and start making a list of things that need to be done.

First things first–Melody hardly has anything in the fridge. I jot down a grocery list and add a note to run by the store later. Then I walk through the apartment, writing down all the things that have to be put together, tidied, or cleaned.

As I suspected, the nursery is basically empty. It has a few unopened boxes and a mountain of diapers, but not much else. I text Damien to see if he can have someone come over and help put all the furniture together. His text back is immediate.

Get her out of the house for a couple of hours, and I'll make sure it gets put together.

I smile as I read the text. He has no reason to help her. He doesn't know her at all, but he cares about me. It's nice to know I can rely on him.

When I finish my list, I sit back down and sip my tea. Melody jerks up in a panic, looking over at May like she's a bomb that's just gone off.

"Is the baby crying?" she asks in a tense voice.

I look over at May, who hasn't even stirred. "She's fine, Mel. I think you're supposed to sleep with she does, right? Everything's fine."

"Nothing is fine!" she whispers hysterically. "Look at this place! It's a disaster. She doesn't even have a real place to sleep."

"I've got it covered." I shrug. "Why don't we get up in a little bit and go to the store? Everything will feel a little better when we get the kitchen restocked."

We probably need a cleaning crew, too.

I quickly text Damien. He just responds with a thumbs up.

"This is a disaster," she groans as her head falls into her hands. "I was supposed to have at least three more weeks! First babies are supposed to come late!"

"We'll get it taken care of, Mel," I assure her.

"And then what?" she shoots back bitterly. "You'll help me for a few days and then you'll get back to your perfect, child-free life while I'm trapped here!"

"Mel," I say as reassuringly as I can. "I'm here to help as long as I can. And you aren't alone in this. Have you talked to your parents?"

She snorts without humor. "They haven't even called."

"I'm sorry," I say sadly.

"It's fine," she cuts in, voice tight. "They made their choice. I made mine."

I want to argue, but I know better. Melody's parents stopped talking to her the second she announced she was pregnant and didn't name the father. They're even more conservative than my parents, which reminds me that they only live forty-five minutes away.

"You can call my parents if you need anything after I leave," I say gently. "I know they're not always easy, but they'll help if you ask. My mom is probably dying to get to spend time with a baby."

She doesn't respond. She just grabs her forgotten mug and takes a long sip.

"This would be better with bourbon," she mutters under her breath, and I pretend not to hear.

I do manage to convince her to take a shower, and we take the baby to the grocery store. I leave a key under the mat for Damien's people, and pray they're done with everything before we get back. I'm seriously concerned that Melody is going to have a breakdown.

Thankfully, grocery shopping takes forever. She literally has nothing in her fridge, and she's hell-bent on eating everything she wasn't allowed to have while she was pregnant. She spends a small fortune on groceries, and by the time we get back to the apartment, it is organized, spotless, and the nursery is set up.

"Harper," she nearly shrieks, causing May to stir unhappily in her car seat. "How did you do all this?"

I just smile and go to the kitchen to put the groceries away. "Let's just say, people care about you."

And even though that isn't technically true, I care about her, and Damien cares about me. I'm sure all the guys would have chipped in if I'd asked, but I need the quickest help possible, and I knew he'd be the one to provide it.

But thinking all that makes me feel guilty that I still haven't told Scott that I'm moving, after all this time. I manage to successfully avoid him for another two days while I help Melody get used to her new normal, but eventually I know I can't keep avoiding him. The longer I put this off, the more my anxiety is going to grow.

It's midafternoon when I finally slip out of Melody's apartment with an excuse about needing to shower and grab clean clothes. I walk two blocks to the coffee shop on the corner, order a latte, and sit on the bench in the warm sun. Then, finally, I make the call.

"Hey, sweet girl," Scott answers, his voice warm and low. "I haven't heard your voice in a while. Texting is great, but it's good to finally hear you. Everything okay with Melody's baby?"

Just hearing his voice makes my chest ache.

"Everything's great!" I say with faux cheer, though I know he can probably hear the tiredness in my voice. May really does cry a lot. "Well, sort of," I amend. "It's been challenging."

"I bet!" he says. "It's good that she has you to help so much. I know you've got a really complicated relationship."

"That's true." I laugh genuinely. "So, listen, I was wondering if you wanted to do dinner tonight."

"Hell yeah, I do!" he whoops. "I'm not going to say no to a night of Harper."

I smile again, soaking in the hot rays of sun. I miss him so much, but I'm also so afraid the news about Paris will ruin everything. I have to savor these moments.

"I can come pick you up if you'd like," he offers when I don't answer him. "What time were you thinking?"

"Maybe six?" I suggest. "I've been covered in baby throw-up for the last few days, so I'll need lots of time to get ready."

"I bet you're still sexy as hell covered in baby vomit," he chuckles. "I'll see you then, baby."

When we hang up, I feel a mixture of relief and reluctance. I really, really hope this isn't the last time I get to enjoy Scott's particular brand of sweetness.

7

———

UNTIL DAWN

The moment I see Harper, an almost territorial growl rumbles in my chest. It's been a few weeks, and she looks good as hell. Her blue dress clings to all of her curves, and I'm dying to get my hands on her.

"Don't you look beautiful," I say as I open the truck door for her, trying to keep up some charade that I'm still a gentleman.

She smiles brightly and gives me a quick peck on the cheek. Hopefully, it's just a taste of things to come. When her body presses into mine, it's all I can do not to pull her against me and plant a big one on her lips.

"So," I say once we're safely on the road, "where are we headed, Miss Ward?"

She glances over with a wry smile. "I was thinking somewhere with food would be good."

I roll my eyes and rest my hand on her exposed thigh. A small shiver runs through her, and damn if I don't want to skip dinner altogether and take her back to my place. I can always make us fresh scrambled eggs after.

"What about that food truck park you were telling me about?" she continues, oblivious to the dirty thoughts brewing in my head.

"That sounds good," I agree, barely paying attention. "Lots of options."

I honestly don't even know how I manage to get us to the food truck park, but somehow, I find myself pulling into the parking lot.

"Maybe some tacos?" Harper suggests, and I let her pull me toward a truck with a long line.

While we wait, she turns to me with the full effect of her gaze, and I get lost in her eyes. But there's something there I don't like. She looks worried, and I just want to smooth the worry lines and kiss it away.

"What's going on, baby?" I ask, concerned.

"I'm going to Paris," she blurts out, and her eyes immediately get glassy.

That is… not what I thought she was going to say.

"Okay," I say slowly. "Like, what, for vacation?"

Damien's probably whisking her away. Figures. He's a great guy, but I wish he realized we don't all have the means to just run off to Paris whenever we want.

"Umm, no," she says carefully, but we're called to place our order before she can say more.

"So," she continues afterward, almost shyly. "I got this job offer to teach at this really fancy art school in Paris, and I decided to take it. But it's just for a semester. For now, anyway."

Before she can blurt out anything else, I kiss her soundly. She's so nervous, and I can't understand it. It's me. She has nothing to be nervous about with me.

When we break apart, she blinks back at me like a deer in headlights.

"That's not the reaction I was expecting," she says breathlessly.

"You seemed nervous," I shrug. "I thought you could use my special brand of comfort."

She wraps her arms around me and presses her body to mine. She reaches up on her tiptoes to kiss me again, deepening it just slightly, though we're both aware we're in public.

"You're right." She smiles when we break away. "That's exactly what I needed."

Our names are called, and the girl in the truck glares at us like she's saying, "Get the hell away from my truck. You're scaring away my customers."

We find a picnic table that's a little away from the crowd and tear into our food.

"So, tell me more," I say excitedly. "This is a huge deal, yeah? My girl is going to be a famous artist!"

"I don't know about all that." She blushes. "I might teach some future famous artists."

"Nah, they'll definitely have your paintings hanging in the–" I stop, realizing I don't know shit about Paris. "What's that fancy museum they have there? The one with the Mona Lisa?"

She giggles, and it's not remotely condescending. She's charmed by me, and I love it. "The Louvre," she tells me. "And I will probably never have a painting there, which is just fine with me. But maybe I'll get to try some new things."

"Damn right, you will!" I say through a bite of my taco. "When do you leave?"

"In three months," she says with a sad sigh.

"That's plenty of time," I tease. "I bet we can break our all-time record."

"In sex or ski ball?" she teases.

"Both, obviously," I answer, sticking my tongue out at her. "But, shit, if you're going to Paris, we better go get you some good sex toys."

She nearly chokes on her drink.

"Excuse me?" she splutters.

I shrug again. "I mean, you won't have me there to satisfy you. We better get you a big daddy with some girth so you don't get too lonely."

She's laughing hysterically now, her face red and tears streaming down her face. This is the version of her I love most, carefree and wild.

"We better get you something too," she purrs when she finally settles down. "I wouldn't want you looking for a new piece of ass while I'm gone."

"You're the only ass I need," I grin at her.

* * *

HARPER

We don't make it past the front door before Scott's lips are on mine, hot and searching.

We're both a little extra turned on by our trip to the sex shop, though we didn't end up buying anything. We'd rather make the most of each other before I go and worry about the logistics later.

My back hits the wall, and I pull him against me, pinning myself between the two. It's the only way I can feel grounded right now. Otherwise, I might simply float away. I'm so ridiculously happy, and I have no idea how I got so lucky.

He's happy for me. He's told me a million times tonight how proud he is of me, and I know he's being genuine. Scott doesn't have a great poker face, so it would be obvious if he were just trying to mask his disappointment.

His hands are on my waist, grabbing at my hips, lingering over my thighs like he can't decide where he wants to touch me most. I know where, but I'm not rushing him. He's made it very clear that he intends to keep me up all night tonight, so I don't push. I let him lead the way.

We stumble into the living room, and it occurs to me how much we get caught here. Tonight, I want it to feel like the first time, so I slowly sink down to my knees and begin unfastening his pants.

"You don't have to, Harper," he groans, in a voice that tells me he very much hopes I will anyway.

"I know," I whisper seductively. "But a toy can't do this."

I unsheathe him from his boxers and slowly wrap my mouth around his tip. He hisses in pleasure as his hand instinctively goes behind my head, his fingers wrapping into my hair.

"No, it certainly can't," he breathes out.

I take him in deeper until I can feel him at the back of my throat. I wrap my hands around what won't fit and give him long, slow strokes, lavishing in how his moans fill the space. They echo around the room so much they wake up Milo, who pads into the room and almost attacks me the second he sees me.

He licks my face happily as I stumble back onto the rug, laughing.

"My dog. My girl. My dog and my girl!" Scott jokes.

"I missed you, too, baby," I say in a high-pitched voice as I scratch Milo lovingly behind the ears. He nuzzles against me, trying to steal me away from Scott.

"Okay, okay," Scott finally says. "That's enough, boy. Let's go out!"

At the sound of his favorite word, Milo's ears go up and he follows Scott out the door as Scott quickly zips his pants back up, cursing underneath his breath.

"Be nice to him," I yell after them, unable to stop the giggle that escapes me.

With Scott gone, I get a wicked idea. I get up and go to his bedroom, where I dig through his drawers for my favorite of his shirts. I quickly strip down to nothing and slip into the shirt. I kick my clothes to the corner of the room where Scott won't immediately notice them and position myself on the bed.

I prop myself up on my elbows and bend one leg, hopefully in a way that looks tempting. I might look absolutely ridiculous, but if Milo doesn't ruin this, I doubt my position on the bed will.

Scott is still grumbling when he comes back in, and I hear him slam the door behind him.

"Where'd you go?" he yells, and I can't help but giggle.

"You'll have to come find me," I call back, butterflies fluttering in my stomach.

When he appears in the bedroom doorway a few seconds later,

he's in nothing but his boxers and a cowboy hat, and I laugh even more.

"Looks like we had a similar idea," I say, eyeing the place where is boxers tent from his erect cock.

I lick my lips subconsciously, and his eyes are glued to them, his pupils dark and large.

"We could be wearing less." He smirks back, stepping out of his boxers and throwing them at me. I catch them easily and throw them onto the pile of my clothes.

"For my collection," I explain when he quirks his eyebrow at me.

"Then it's only fair I take a pair of yours," he says, running his fingers underneath the hem of his shirt. His eyes go wide when he realizes I'm bare. "I can just get them later."

He nearly growls as he climbs on top of me, quickly pulling the shirt over my head.

"Fuck, you're beautiful," he breathes raggedly. "You'll definitely have to leave me some pictures for my spank bank."

"I promise," I whisper as I pull him down for a deep, passionate kiss.

There's no time for preamble. We're both ready, and we can't risk another unfortunate interruption. He quickly slips into me, stretching me wide in the way that only he can. I arch into him, wanting to swallow him into me.

But his movements are unhurried. He lavishes me with long, hot kisses, moving at an achingly slow rhythm while our hands explore each other. He wasn't kidding about going till dawn, but at this rate, we'll only get one round in. I giggle at the thought, and that seems to encourage him.

"You're going to shatter me, Harper," he says sweetly. "And I think I want you to."

I kiss him hard, urging him to move faster, to go even deeper. And he does. Our bodies create a rhythm that is wholly, completely ours.

Then I'm on all fours and he's entering me from behind. Then, somehow, we end up back in the rug, and I'm on top of him, saving a horse and riding a cowboy. Milo is sound asleep, and when we both shatter for the fifth or sixth time, he barely raises his head, as if he's sick of us.

Blearily, we do end up watching the sun come up together, wrapped in each other's arms. I hold on to him tightly, remembering that in a few months, we'll be watching the sun rise hours apart.

8

THE MOST ROMANTIC WEEK

Harper

Summer flies by fast and hectic, like a tornado. Every morning I wake up with a new mental checklist: Make sure my passport is updated, work on my lesson plans, respond to the school about my apartment. Some days my list includes helping Melody, sending her articles on breast pumps, watching the baby so she can do a yoga class. I live in constant motion, and still it feels like I'm always behind.

Even so, I'm happier than I've ever been, and I'm not even in Paris yet. I'm emotional all the time, and exhausted, and usually overstimulated, but still, I'm happy.

May is such an incredible baby, and I love spending time with her. Every time I hold her and get a hit of her baby smell, my heart melts a little more. I'm still worried about Mel, but I remind myself that I have to focus on my life and leave her life to her. It's hard, but I think she's getting the hang of things, and that helps me let go.

I split myself like a calendar, trying to give everyone what they need, while storing up all the memories I can before I go. Scott and I spend slow days together on the farm, moving through sun-drenched hours with our hands tangled in sheets and our feet bare in the grass. We harvest peaches and make out in the barn. We bathe Milo and milk cows, and I know I'm going to miss all of it when I'm gone.

Tomás tries to keep me plied with cultural experiences, taking me dancing and to art openings, and reading a book by Pablo Neruda to me in Spanish. He keeps making jokes that he doesn't want me to turn into a French snob, so he wants to keep my experiences balanced. I promise him I'll try to find a salsa club in Paris, and if I can't, I'll take a quick trip to Spain.

Rafe and I don't get as much time as I would like. He's in pre-season training, and he's busy so much of the time. The stolen moments we get together are full of passion and making up for lost time, both past and future. There's also a comfort between us that is so reminiscent of our long history. Sometimes, he just comes over after practice and lays his head on my lap while I watch TV at the end of the day.

Damien gives me a little more space, since he has more of an opportunity to visit me in Paris. He's planned out our week visit there to the last second. I'm a little intimidated by our itinerary, but he assures me that I'll be grateful for all the insight when I'm on my own.

I help McKenzy find a subletter for the apartment, but she says she's excited to have the studio to herself for three whole months. I can't wait to see what incredible pieces she finishes while I'm in Paris.

Too soon, the summer draws to a close, and then August hits. My bags are packed, my to-do lists are completely done, and Damien is driving me to his private jet for our week together in Paris.

To say I'm nervous is the understatement of the year. When I first got the offer, I was terrified of telling the guys. Then, I was so busy with Melody and getting ready, I didn't have the space to really consider what I'm doing. Now, though, as we pull up to the airstrip, the self-doubt is starting to creep in.

What if I'm a terrible teacher?

"You're overthinking this," Damien says, and I shoot him a glare.

"I knew you were a mind reader," I tease.

"No, I'm just exceptionally good at reading your face," he answers without looking up from his phone. "You look stressed, which means you're probably stuck in a loop of insecure thoughts. You don't need to be scared, little red bird. They're lucky to have you."

I nod and take a deep breath, even though I don't believe it. The driver loads up all of my suitcases onto the plane, which is one amazing benefit of flying privately. I didn't have to worry about packing limits. When we board the plane, there's another bouquet of irises and a bottle of champagne chilling on ice.

I turn to Damien with my eyebrow quirked.

"This is just more celebration," he shrugs. "Don't read so much into it."

"I'm not giving up my psychic theory," I say, reaching up to kiss him.

The plane ride is a blur of good champagne, good food, and really good sex. Damien also makes me sleep so I'm ready to hit the ground running. When we arrive. I'm glad, because the moment we land, a private car takes us to my new apartment.

It's absolutely adorable. It's small, but full of classic European charm. The school arranged it all, but Damien keeps grumbling that he can find me a much nicer penthouse in a fancier part of the city. I just roll my eyes and start unpacking. I'm already obsessed with this little space that will become my home for the next few months.

The school has left the fridge stocked, and I notice there are a few extras that I didn't ask for, like my favorite wine and a vase of sunflowers.

"You're incorrigible," I complain to Damien, but in response, he just leads me to the bedroom and we christen the new bed.

That night, we go out to dinner at a gorgeous Michelin-starred restaurant right near the Eiffel Tower. We take a walk to the tower afterward, and I take a million pictures.

We walk along the Seine, and then he guides me into a jazz club in a hidden alleyway with a low ceiling and an intimate atmosphere. We drink more wine and he mindlessly strokes my leg as we listen to the music. By the time we get back to my place, I'm so horny I nearly rip my dress off.

The next day, he takes me to an old bookstore that has been run by the same owner for over sixty years. She refuses to alphabetize anything, but when Damien asks her for a specific book, she knows exactly where it is. It's cramped and crowded, full of volumes of rare old books and gorgeous hardback covers. Damien buys me a copy of Pride and Prejudice in French.

We walk everywhere because Damien says it's the Parisian way. This surprises me, since I'm used to him having us chauffeured everywhere. My feet ache by day three, but I don't complain. I don't want to miss a thing. He buys me pain au chocolat in the mornings and wine in the afternoons, and at night we sit on the balcony of my apartment and listen to the city hum.

"I get it now," I whisper one night, watching the rooftops turn blue in the twilight.

"Get what?"

"Why people are so in love with Paris."

He smiles faintly.

"Even the hot nights manage to be romantic." I rest my head on his shoulder. "Will you come back and visit me while I'm here?'

"As often as I can," he says without hesitation. "And if you ever need me, just call me and I'll be on the next jet out."

We make out all over the city. I don't mean to be so prolific with my PDA, but it's the City of Love, after all. Sometimes he pulls me into alleyways and pushes me up against the wall, but often he'll just kiss me right in the middle of a café or an art gallery. It's intoxicating to be so open with our relationship here, but every now and then, I'll catch the flash of a camera.

It's easy to forget sometimes who Damien is. He's an internationally known billionaire. He's graced the cover of magazines and is often debated about on social media. When I'm with him, he's just my hot, rich boyfriend, but to the rest of the world, he's Damien Blackwood, corporate genius. When I see camera flashes, though, it can be sobering.

One night, we're dancing in some tucked-away club in the eleventh arrondissement. The music is thumping, the air thick with heat, rhythm, and alcohol, and my body is pressed against his. My dress riding a little too high on my thighs, his mouth against my neck, and I'm laughing happily when a flash catches me off guard.

I stiffen a little, but Damien doesn't notice right away. His hand is on my hip, his mouth trailing toward mine, and I let myself melt again. It's not like I'm going to chase after the person, and what can I do about it anyway? But it leaves a bad taste in my mouth.

I saw someone taking our picture outside a bistro two days ago. Another snapped a shot while we were sitting on a bench by the river, and my head was on Damien's shoulder. I even caught a man ducking behind a stack of oranges at a produce stall while we kissed outside a bakery.

Apparently, people recognize us now. Pretty soon, they may start recognizing me.

"Hey," I murmur against his ear after a few more minutes of dancing. "I think we've been made."

Damien leans back slightly, his brows raised. "Define 'made.'"

"Someone took our picture," I explain.

He doesn't look remotely bothered by this news. He just pulls me even closer. "Then I hope they got my good side."

"They always do," I mutter, cringing a bit.

He brushes his thumb over my cheek. "Are you upset?"

I hesitate, but decide to be honest. "A little."

"Do you want to go back to your place?"

"No," I say hesitantly. "But I think I need some air."

He nods and grabs my hand, leading us out of the nightclub and back out to the street. We walk for a while with his arm draped protectively around my shoulder, and I try not to let my worries get the best of me.

I'm just not used to being watched, that's all. I don't love the idea of being someone's headline. I really don't love the idea of my parents seeing me kissing someone else in public. But I remind myself that we're not in Minneapolis. We're not in the U.S.A. at all. These are

European tabloids. They're in French. I doubt my parents will see them.

Still, the thought lingers.

Would they lose their minds if they saw me kissing Damien in a Parisian nightclub? Almost certainly.

Would they judge me for swaying against his body like I belong there? Without question.

Still, that doesn't stop me from letting Damien pull me against him. I don't mind when he kisses me gently and promises to always protect me.

We take a day trip to Nice and spend the afternoon drinking red wine with seafood pasta at a place with checkered tablecloths and barely functioning fans. The salty breeze smells heavily of garlic. Damien keeps feeding me olives off his fork, and I'm pretty sure I never want to leave Italy, teaching job be damned.

That night, there's a little music festival in the next town over. We find ourselves dancing in the middle of a square under strings of lights while an accordion player winks at me and Damien spins me like it's the 1940s. I laugh so hard I can't breathe.

Another day, we hop a train to Switzerland, where the mountains look painted, and the air is clean. We tour a family-run chocolate shop, where I eat so much I'm sure I'm going to explode. We sample cheese with names I can't pronounce and get mildly lost trying to find a lookout point that ends up being a field of wildflowers that makes me feel like I'm in *The Sound of Music*.

It is the most romantic week of my entire life, but like all things, it has to come to an end, eventually.

The morning Damien leaves, the sky is overcast. He's already dressed with his suitcase packed, and his car is on the way. I sit on the edge of my bed, watching him do one last check of his briefcase.

"Are you sure you have everything?" I ask, even though I know he does.

He looks over and smiles faintly. "Everything but you."

"I'll be okay," I say. "Go be brilliant."

"You promise to call if you need me?"

"Only if you promise to get here as soon as you can."

He walks over, cups my face in his hands, and kisses me with so much enthusiasm I almost forget he has to leave. "I'll be back soon," he murmurs. "You won't even have time to miss me."

"I'll miss you anyway."

He touches his forehead to mine. "Then miss me well."

9

────────

WHAT A WAY TO END THE DAY

I barely get any sleep the night before my first day. I'm not nervous exactly; I've just got so much energy that I can't force my mind to calm down. It feels like I've been holding my breath all summer, and I finally have the chance to exhale.

When I walk out onto the street, the early morning air smells like fresh pastries and espresso. This, I could definitely get used to. I step onto the sidewalk in front of my apartment and glance up at the pink-tinged sky. Paris is just waking up with me, and the city is still quiet. It reminds me of being a kid on the first day of school. Just like then, it's still too early for most people to be out and about, but I'm on a mission to start my new year.

I take the Metro one stop too far by accident, but I don't mind walking the extra blocks. It gives me a chance to pass by a patisserie with giant pistachio croissants. I make a mental note to stop on the way home, if I'm not so exhausted I don't remember.

The school sits on a quiet street lined with tall trees and buildings that look like they've stood here for centuries. It's beautiful in that quintessential Paris way, full of wrought-iron balconies and aged stone. The brass plaque beside the door reads 'École des Beaux-Arts de Paris,' and the nerves finally hits me.

This is happening. I'm actually doing this.

The lobby is cool and elegant, which does little to ease my nerves. A woman with short gray hair and a linen scarf greets me and directs me to the administrative wing, where I'm supposed to meet my new boss, André. I say his name silently in my head a few times the way she said it. The emphasis on the last "e" and not the "A" the way it is in the USA.

When I knock on his office door, a kind voice tells me to "entrer."

He's younger than I expected him to be, possibly in his early forties, though he could be younger than that. He's thin, but the tightness of his shirt speaks to a toned body. His warm brown skin and wire-rimmed glasses give him a slightly academic air. He's wearing navy trousers and a crisp white shirt with no tie, and he looks up from a stack of papers with a charming smile.

"Harper Ward," he says in a thick accent as he stands to shake my hand. "Welcome. I'm glad you made it."

"Thank you," I say, returning his smile. "I'm so excited to be here."

He gestures for me to sit, and I do, already relieved by the easy energy in the room.

"I saw one of your pieces in Chicago," he says, steepling his fingers as he leans forward slightly. "There was a gallery show with emerging American artists, and one of your pieces caught my attention. It had… um, these fragmented faces. In blue?"

"Fracture," I say, surprised and a little flattered that he remembers it. "That was part of a collection I did last spring."

"Yes. It had depth. Not just technically, but emotionally. I thought, this is someone who's seeing things in a new way. And we're overdue for new eyes here."

I blink, thrown by the compliment but trying to stay composed.

"That means a lot," I answer quietly. "Thank you."

He waves it off.

"We're not expecting you to reinvent the curriculum overnight," he says with a smile. "But I hope you'll feel comfortable enough to add your own perspective. You'll be teaching the intermediate-level studio course. It's mostly second-years, and a few very talented first-years. It's a good place to start."

"I've already put together lesson plans," I tell him. "They're a little flexible, since I want to get a sense of where the students are skill-wise. But I've mapped out about six weeks of instruction to start."

"Excellent. That's more preparation than some instructors do in a semester." He chuckles before standing and moving toward the door. "Come, I'll show you your classroom."

The hallways are wide and echo softly beneath our steps. There's natural light everywhere, thanks to enormous arched windows, and I find myself glancing out at the city every chance I get.

André gestures to a door with a frosted glass panel. Inside is a studio space that looks like it belongs in a film. It has tall ceilings, rows of easels, well-worn stools, and paint-splattered worktables. There's a wide sink in the back corner, and a supply closet better stocked than most hobby stores I've been to back home.

"This is yours," he tells me.

I walk in slowly, trailing my fingers along the edge of one of the tables. It smells like linseed oil and dust. So many stories are going to start at these tables. So much art is going to be made here. I don't realize I'm smiling until André chuckles softly behind me.

"Good?" he asks.

"Very," I breathe.

He gives me a quick nod.

"Your first class is Monday morning. Today is yours to settle in, set up, make the space yours. There's coffee in the faculty lounge. And you'll find your ID and office keys in the top drawer."

"Thank you so much," I say again, not sure how many times I've said it now but unable to help myself.

He leaves me with a final "bonne chance," and I'm alone. I turn in a slow circle, taking it all in.

Standing in the middle of this incredible space, I feel the quiet nudge of inspiration. This is a workshop that most artists would drool over, and it's all mine. Well, mine and a handful of intermediate art students.

I unpack my messenger bag and pull out the small notebook where I've been keeping ideas for both my own pieces and my lesson plans. I flip to the last sketch I did on the plane and tear it out carefully, pinning it to the cork board by the supply cabinet. Then I reach into the closet, grab a canvas, and lean it on one of the easels.

I don't have time to paint now, but the tools are there as soon as I am. It makes me want to rush through my setup just to get back to it, but my students deserve more.

By midmorning, I've rearranged the stools and checked the inventory list against the supplies in the cabinet. I scribble down what's missing and email the studio manager with a few requests, like extra charcoal, fresh gesso, and a better fan. It's warm in here, and I'm already sweating through my linen top. It's a shame central air conditioning isn't common in France.

I take a break just before noon and make my way to the lounge. The faculty kitchen is more or less what I expected, although the fancy espresso machine is sight for sore eyes. A few teachers sit around a circular table, laughing in quick French that I can barely follow.

One of the women waves me over when she sees me hesitating.

"You must be Harper," she says brightly, in English. She's in her early thirties, with short copper hair and a thick Parisian accent. "I'm Élodie. I teach sculpture."

I introduce myself, and before I can sit down, someone else pulls out a chair for me. The rest of the faculty members introduce themselves between bites of salad and coffee. There's Julien, who teaches drawing, and Camille, who handles art history. A couple of others pop in and out, including someone from the design department who has blue paint in her hair and doesn't seem to notice.

Everyone is kind. They ask me where I'm from, how I like the city so far, and if I've found the best *boulangerie* yet. I tell them I'm still searching and that it feels impossible to pick just one. They make the loneliness I've been feeling start to ease in my chest.

Unfortunately, it doesn't go away completely. When I get back to my quiet apartment, I'm suddenly reminded of exactly how alone I am here.

I kick off my shoes by the door and wander toward the kitchen, toeing the edge of the rug as I pass. Outside, the sun is still hanging low in the sky, casting buttery light through the gauzy curtains. There's a hum of life beyond the windows, but in here, it's just me.

I drop my keys into a little ceramic dish I bought at the market yesterday. It clinks against the change in my pocket, and the sound feels absurdly loud.

The day went better than I could've hoped, but now that I'm alone again, the buzz of excitement wears off. I open the fridge, take out a bottle of sparkling water, and lean against the counter while I drink it straight.

I could paint, journal, or organize the reference books the school gave me. Instead, I let myself sink onto the couch and pull my phone out of my pocket. I open the group chat, scroll past a few memes Rafe sent and a grainy picture of Milo that Scott posted earlier.

There's a tug deep in my chest as I stare at the photo.

God, I miss Scott. I miss his voice and his hands and his smell. I miss his stupid jokes and the way he looks at me. I open our thread and hover over the video call button for a second before tapping it.

It only rings once before his face fills the screen.

"Hey, baby," he says, grinning. "Damn, Paris suits you."

My breath catches. He's in a white tank top, his hair damp like he just got out of the shower.

"That shirt suits you," I say lowly. "But you should take it off."

His smile softens, and his eyes crinkle at the corners.

"That isn't a bad idea," he chuckles. "It's been hot as hell here the last few days."

"I wish you were here," I say softly.

His tongue darts out to wet his bottom lip.

"I'd do unspeakable things to you if I were," he says with a slow grin.

I laugh, but it's a breathy sound, my pulse starting to pick up. "Oh, yeah?" I ask, playing along, voice just a little silkier. "What kind of things?"

He leans back slightly with one arm resting behind his head. His tank top rides up just enough to show a strip of tanned stomach. His eyes scan me slowly through the screen.

"First, I'd sit right down on that couch with you. I wouldn't even kiss you right away. I'd just look at you for a minute, touch your leg, let my fingers trace up that soft skin behind your knee."

I shift, suddenly hyperaware of exactly where he means.

"I'd make you wait," he continues, voice lower now, thicker. "Make you say please."

"Please," I whisper, breath catching.

He groans, rubbing his jaw. "Take your shirt off." He parrots my earlier command, but I actually listen.

I swallow and tug the loose top over my head, revealing the lacy white bralette I'm wearing under it.

Scott lets out a slow whistle. "Fuck, baby."

He adjusts the camera so I can see more of him. He's sprawled on the bed now, his muscles taut and his eyes locked on me. "Take all of it off," he says. "Let me see you."

I slip the bralette over my head, bare now, the warm air of the apartment brushing across my skin.

Scott's hand is already slipping beneath the waistband of his jeans.

"Touch yourself," I tell him, bolder now, the desire spreading through me like fire.

He unbuttons his jeans and pushes them down enough for me to see the way he's already hard. He wraps his hand around himself slowly, deliberately. "I've been thinking about you all day," he murmurs. "I kept replaying that last night we had before you left. You really rode me like a cowboy."

I slide one hand down my stomach, between my thighs, and gasp at how wet I already am. "Keep going," I whisper, my voice barely a breath.

"You were so greedy for me," he says, stroking himself, slow and tight. "I didn't think I was gonna last. But you took me in deep like the hungry girl you are."

I slip two fingers inside myself and moan, the sound too loud in the quiet apartment. "I miss the way you feel," I say. "The way you stretch me, how you always fill me up just right."

Scott groans, his hips lifting off the bed. "Show me," he pants. "Let me see you."

I angle the camera down just enough to give him a view of my hand between my thighs, my body arching to get more friction.

"Jesus, Harper," he says, eyes wide with hunger. "You're so fucking beautiful when you touch yourself like that."

I can't speak anymore. My breath is coming fast and shallow. I watch him stroke himself, eyes never leaving mine.

"I'm so close," I whisper.

"Come for me," he growls. "Right now, baby. Let me see you fall apart."

I cry out as pleasure crashes over me. My back arches off the couch, and my fingers dig into the fabric, trying to find purchase. I ride it out in shudders, my body shaking as I gasp his name over and over again. He follows right after, groaning loud and deep, his chest rising and falling like he's just run a mile.

We both lie there, panting, the screens still filled with each other's flushed, satisfied faces.

I reach for the blanket and drape it over my lap.

"That's one hell of a way to end a first day of work," I say with a giggle when I finally catch my breath.

Scott laughs at my bad joke, grinning at me happily.

"Unfortunately, I still have a few more hours of work to do," he groans. "But this was definitely a nice afternoon delight. I miss you, baby."

"I miss you, too," I say before letting him go.

And then I'm back in my empty apartment, with nothing to keep the loneliness at bay.

1 0

———

ALONE

Harper

I'm so giddy as I walk to my classroom for my first ever session, I can almost hear it in the bright way my heels clack against the old tiles. I open the door to find my students already assembled, some chatting with each other, while others stare seriously at their hands while they wait for class to start.

I try not to be intimidated by how effortlessly cool they all look. They're all so Parisian. There's no other way to put it.

They all seem so unbothered by anything going on around them, so I try to employ the same strategy. I go to my desk and begin introductions. I'm pleased to find that a handful of my students are international, so maybe I'm not the only one who's just pretending to be unbothered.

We spend a good portion of the class going over the syllabus before I start my first lecture. They listen intently and engage with the material, which is the best result I could have possibly asked for.

But best of all, they ask incredibly intelligent questions. They seem excited about the direction we're taking with this course, and I assure them that we're going to be doing plenty of painting over the course of the semester. I end the lecture by asking them to share their favorite materials to work with, and once it's over, I finally release a long breath.

I survived. I got through my first lesson, and it was actually really fun.

I still have a lot to learn. I talked too fast. I lost track of time during the lecture. One student asked for a material I'd never heard of, and I made a note to look it up later and act like I totally knew what it was all along. But I think I could be good at this. I think I could love it.

I stay behind in the studio for a while, wiping charcoal off the tables and letting the satisfaction of the day settle in. I deserve to be happy here. I could be really happy here.

On the way home, I stop at the patisserie and buy that pistachio croissant I promised myself I would. The woman behind the counter smiles at me and compliments my earrings. At least, I think that's what she says. French is still a huge learning curve for me.

I take the long way back, down the Seine, watching the golden light bounce off the water. Every bridge I pass looks like it's part of a movie set—lovers hold hands, pigeons flutter near café tables, and the air smells like sugar and bread and the most delicious concoctions.

Everything here is so magical.

I want to paint everything, from the curve of the balconies to the way the sunlight glints off damp cobblestones. The city feels alive in a way I've never experienced. And I don't just want to observe it. I want to capture it forever in oils and acrylics.

This must be how every great artist has felt about Paris. I know that I'm not special in my feelings of the place, but that doesn't dampen the excitement in any way.

When I finally reach my apartment, I'm practically buzzing with an energy that can only be satisfied by a paintbrush in my hand. I spend the early evening sketching at the kitchen table with the windows open and my music playing low. I draw a little boy I saw earlier with chocolate all over his face, and I let the lines flow until they almost dance on the page. I forget to eat dinner, but that doesn't matter. I'm used to ignoring my hunger pangs for the sake of art.

When I'm finally satisfied with my work for the evening, I curl up on the couch with a cup of mint tea and scroll through the messages from the guys. Tomas sent a photo of his dinner, some kind of farm-to-table masterpiece with edible flowers that Scott made fun of. Damien replied with a GIF of Gordon Ramsay looking impressed, and Rafe sent a thumbs-up emoji. He's probably right in the middle of practice.

They're all so ridiculous, and I love them. For a moment, I let myself imagine what it would be like if they were all here with me. We could walk the streets together, get wine-drunk in the Latin Quarter, kiss in front of the Eiffel Tower like tourists.

I fall asleep with those images in my head, wishing they could all be here with me. But a call at 2:16 A.M. pulls me from that magical dream.

I'm groggy and half-asleep, disoriented by the darkness, but I grab my phone from the nightstand without thinking.

I answer with a sleepy, "Hello?" without thinking to check the caller ID. Everyone important knows that I'm in Paris, and they know there's a pretty significant time change. Whoever is calling must have something important to tell me.

"Harper Ann Ward, do you have any idea how humiliating it is to open your email and see your daughter making a spectacle of herself across the internet?"

I sit up too fast, my heart slamming. I should have checked the caller ID.

"Mom?" I ask blearily. "What are you talking about?"

"Don't play dumb, young lady. You know exactly what I'm talking about. A friend from church forwarded me an article. A tabloid article, Harper. With pictures."

My stomach knots. Pictures of what, exactly? This could be incredibly bad.

My voice is dry when I ask, "What pictures?"

"Don't pretend you don't know. You were dancing with some

man. Kissing him! And now you're on gossip sites being labeled some kind of jet-setting party girl. Is that how you want to represent yourself? Is that how you want to represent me?"

I close my eyes, dragging in a slow breath through my nose.

"It was a private party," I say. "Someone must've taken a picture without my knowledge. It wasn't meant for—"

"And do you want to know what every single comment under the article said? 'Who is this mystery woman?' That's what they're calling you! Mystery woman! Well, I know who the mystery woman is. It's my daughter!"

She spits the last sentence like it burns her tongue.

I run a hand over my face. "Mom—"

"How could you be so promiscuous, Harper?" she demands. "How could you do this to Rafe? What on earth is he going to think when he sees these pictures?"

It's the word "promiscuous" that really sends me over the edge. Like I've suddenly become a character in a Lifetime movie about fallen daughters and judgmental mothers.

"It's two in the morning," I say, my voice flat. "I'm in Paris. You couldn't wait until daylight to call and scream at me?"

"Oh, I'm sorry my moral concern didn't come with a time zone converter."

I press my fingertips into my temple, trying to hold on to the part of me that spent the day teaching actual students and walking through an actual dream city and eating a croissant that could make grown men cry. But she's steamrolling all of it with her outrage.

"I should really go back to sleep," I say, softer now. "I'll call you in the morning when we can talk like adults."

"Adults don't behave like this, Harper."

I don't answer.

"I just–" She sighs, and for a second I think I hear something real under the edge. "I just don't understand you anymore."

"I'm not asking you to," I whisper. "I'm just asking you to love me anyway."

But she doesn't say it. She doesn't say I love you, or I'm proud of you, or even to be safe.

She just hangs up.

And I'm left staring at the dark screen of my phone, my heart pounding and my throat tight, the walls of this beautiful little Paris apartment suddenly feeling a whole lot closer.

I want to cry. I want to laugh. I want to throw something through the damn window.

Instead, I lie back down and stare at the ceiling, replaying the whole conversation on a loop like some kind of emotional horror movie.

I should've been prepared for something like this to happen. I did see that photographer in Barcelona, after all. I just didn't think this kind of news would get back to the States. I shouldn't have underestimated my mother's busy-body friends.

I think about how it'll look to them. To the women at church who raised their eyebrows when I cut my hair short in tenth grade. To the neighbors who still think I'm going to come home and marry some Midwestern dentist and have three well-behaved kids in a cul-de-sac.

Let them talk.

I curl deeper into the blankets, still wide awake, still buzzing with hurt.

Let them all talk.

They don't know what it's like to be kissed by Rafe when his whole world is falling apart and he still manages to make me feel like I'm the only thing keeping him together. They don't know how Tomas says 'mi amor' like it's a prayer, or how Damien looks at me like I'm the most precious thing in a room full of priceless art. They'll never understand how Scott holds me so gently after a day working hard on the farm.

They don't know love, not the way I do. Not the way we do.

So, no, I'm not cheating. I'm not hiding. I'm not ashamed.

But I am tired of being misunderstood, of fighting for space in my life, of explaining joy to people who don't want to understand it.

Eventually, I grab my phone and scroll through the messages

again, looking for a lifeline.

Scott's name glows back at me.

Me: Apparently, I'm a scandal now.

Scott: What did you do this time? ;)

Me: US Weekly published photos of me kissing Rafe and dancing with Damien. My mom is convinced I've destroyed my soul and betrayed Rafe all in one night.

Scott: Tell your mom we're all wildly in love with you and fully consenting.

Me: Is that you volunteering to call her?

Scott: Absolutely not. From what I've heard, that woman is terrifying. I've had nightmares, and I've never even met her.

That makes me laugh, and the pressure in my chest eases, just a little.

Scott: Seriously though, are you okay?

Me: Not really.

Scott: Want me to fly out and throw your phone into the Seine?

I laugh again at this. But that would just delay the inevitable.

Me: Tempting. But no.

Scott: Do you want to talk about it?

I pause, my fingers hovering over the keyboard. I do want to talk about it, but not through a screen. Not even over the phone. I want to be lying in bed with him, hiding under the covers as he comforts me.

I want his voice. His arms. His heartbeat under my cheek. But that's a luxury I don't get to have right now.

Me: Maybe tomorrow. I just needed to feel less alone.

Scott: You're never alone, Harp. Not for one second.

I stare at that message for a long time, blinking back the tears that finally come.

Because Scott loves me. And Tomas loves me. And Rafe and Damien love me. But I can't tell my mother any of this. How would I possibly explain to my mother that Rafe wouldn't care if he saw pictures of me kissing Damien, because he already knows about it?

It's a thought that keeps me up tossing and turning for the rest of the night.

11

WORRISOME CALLS

Harper

It's only mid-morning when my phone lights up with "Mom" across the screen. My stomach clenches on reflex. It's been a couple of days since her middle-of-the-night beratement of my character. I exhale sharply as I decide if I want to answer it. But I know if I let it go to voicemail, it'll only make things worse. I slide my thumb across the screen and put the phone to my ear.

"Hey, Mom."

She clears her throat, and I hear the tension in her voice.

"Hi, honey."

She actually sounds calm, so maybe this will be okay.

"Hi," I say slowly. "What's up?"

"I, um," she starts. "I wanted to apologize for the other night."

I sit on the edge of my bed, the phone pressed tight against my ear.

"Really?" I try not to sound so surprised, but I can't help it. My mother has never apologized for anything ever.

"Yes," she sighs. "I was upset. I saw those pictures online and just lost it. That wasn't fair of me."

The tightness I've had in my chest since her first call eases just a little. "Thank you for saying that."

"I shouldn't have called you so late, either. I didn't think about the time difference."

"No, you didn't," I agree, but I'm careful to keep my voice even. I don't want to set her off again. "Listen," I say carefully. "I want us to be able to talk. I do. But my love life is off limits."

"Harper–"

"I'm serious," I cut her off, gently but firmly. "You don't have to like it. But you don't get to weigh in on it anymore. It's not up for discussion." I wait, biting my lip.

She finally lets out a tired sigh. "Fine."

I almost smile. Maybe it's not enthusiastic approval, but it's acceptance. That's just about the best I could ever ask of her. "Thank you."

She doesn't respond for a minute, then she clears her throat again. My stomach knots again in anticipation of whatever hammer she's about to drop.

"Anyway," she continues, her voice shifting from apologetic to thoughtful. "That's not actually why I was calling."

"Oh?" I feign nonchalance, even though I am beyond curious.

"I need to talk to you about Melody."

My heart immediately falls into my stomach. I've been so worried about her, and this confirms all my fears. "What's going on with her?" I ask.

"She's been leaving the baby here," my mother answers immediately, like the answer was already loaded on her tongue. "A lot."

I wince. I knew Melody was struggling, but there's a difference between asking for support and taking advantage. "Like how much?"

"Well," she says, and I can hear her walking around, the floorboards creaking underfoot. "She drops May off in the morning and sometimes doesn't pick her up until after dinner. Some nights she asks if May can just sleep over so she can get some rest."

I pinch the bridge of my nose to stave off the impending headache. "Is she working yet?"

"Not really," Mom says, and I can hear the frown in her voice.

"She's not back at her old job yet. I think she might be freelancing a little, but Harper, I don't think she's doing well."

My heart aches for Melody. I knew things weren't easy for her when I left, but I didn't imagine she would be struggling this much.

"What do you mean?" I ask, not feeling very confident about my mother's definition of 'not doing well.'

"She seems flat and disconnected. Melody is tired all the time. She's stopped bringing May over with all the cute little things she used to pack. Half the time, I end up giving May a bath here because she clearly hasn't been bathed."

I rake my free hand through my hair. "Have you talked to Melody about it?"

"I've tried to," she admits. "But you know how she is. She brushes me off. She tells me she's fine and that she's just tired. But it seems a lot more serious than just tiredness."

The words "postpartum depression" pop into my head, and I ache for her even more. Poor Melody. "Mom," I say quietly. "She might need some professional help."

"I know," she says in a small voice. "That's why I wanted to tell you. She isn't listening to me, but she might listen to you."

"Okay," I breathe, nodding to myself. "I'll call her and see what I can do."

She sighs in relief. "Thank you."

We're both silent for a moment, both a little unsure about how to navigate this new stalemate.

"You don't mind watching the baby though, right?" I finally ask gently.

"Oh God, no." Her voice softens immediately. "You know I adore that baby. I love having her here. I just want her mother to be okay too."

My eyes sting at her words. It's a genuinely lovely thing for my mom to say. "Thank you for taking care of her," I say earnestly.

"You don't have to thank me for that," she responds just as kindly.

But I really do. It's more than I expected her to do.

When we finally hang up, I stare at the ceiling for a minute, trying to steady my breathing. It's better. It's progress. But it's also a reminder of everything I've left behind at home.

I text Melody that afternoon: Hey. Can we talk soon? Just want to check in.

She doesn't respond.

The next day, I'm standing in the teachers' break room at school, trying to shake off the conversation with my mom, when I realize I'm just standing there staring at the coffee pot like it's going to brew itself. I finally shake myself and pour a cup.

I take a sip of coffee and immediately wince. It's too hot. I'm blowing gently on the rim when I hear the door open behind me. I glance back over my shoulder and see the handsome teacher I've noticed the last few days.

He's tall with messy brown hair that looks intentional. He has faint laugh lines around his mouth and a hint of stubble. His eyes are such a warm brown, I swear they could melt chocolate. He smiles at me, completely unaware of me cataloging his physical appearance.

"Bonjour," he says kindly.

"Bonjour," I reply, trying to sound casual, even though my heart does this ridiculous little thump-thump in my chest.

"It's Harper, right?" he asks. "You're the American teacher."

"That's me," I giggle.

I actually giggle. I feel like a complete idiot.

He moves a little closer, enough that I catch the clean scent of his aftershave.

"I'm Lucas," he says, offering me his hand to shake.

His palm is warm and a little rough.

"It's nice to officially meet you," I say, trying for casual.

"Likewise," he says with a grin. "I've seen you around. I thought I should introduce myself before it got any more awkward."

I laugh again, trying for a less girly sound this time.

"That's a good idea," I affirm.

He leans casually against the counter and glances at me sideways. "So," he starts, blowing on his coffee. "How are you finding Paris?"

My lips twist wryly. "It's intimidating," I admit. "But beautiful. And very expensive."

He laughs, and the sound is so genuinely amused it makes my skin warm. "You've got us down," he says, pushing a stray lock of hair off his forehead. "You're teaching the intermediate painting, yes?"

I nod.

He gestures at himself. "I teach sculpting."

"Ah," I say, taking another cautious sip of coffee. "A chisel man."

He snorts. "That's one way to put it," he laughs, setting down his own cup. "Listen, if you're interested, I could show you around sometime. Properly. Not the tourist stuff. The real Paris."

He pulls a small, folded piece of paper from his pocket and finds a pen on one of the tables. He scribbles something on it before handing it to me. "Here."

I take it automatically. It's his Instagram handle.

"Message me anytime," he says.

Our fingers brush as I take the paper, and I swear there's a tiny spark of electricity. My face flushes hot. I see it register in his expression, too. He just holds my gaze for an extra heartbeat before giving me a polite nod.

"Well," he says, almost sadly. "I should probably get back. Sculpting isn't going to teach itself."

I chuckle, feeling oddly breathless. "Thank you," I say, lifting the paper a little in almost a salute.

He gives me one last warm smile before slipping out the door.

When I finish teaching for the day, it seems wrong to go back home. It's such a lovely evening, and the city seems to be calling me. So, I let myself drift aimlessly, exploring on my own. I walk past the old, regal buildings that drip with history. I pass by buskers playing accordions and violins. I walk by flower shops with buckets overflowing onto the pavement in bursts of color.

Eventually, hunger leads me to a tiny bistro on a side street a few blocks from my apartment.

Outside are wobbly tables and mismatched chairs. I sit down, and a waitress hands me a peeling menu. This feels like the authentic

Parisian experience. I ordered a kir, a French cocktail with white wine and liqueur, and a simple sandwich. I don't even care much about what's on it, because the bread here is so divine that I barely notice the meats and cheeses.

I watch the bustle on the street while I sip my drink and wait for my food. Couples walk by holding hands, groups of friends laugh with each other, and a few tables over I see a waiter flirting shamelessly with a group of girls.

Out of nowhere, loneliness grips me. Here I am in the most beautiful city in the world, and I'm all alone. This should be the best experience of my life, but I just want to be home with the people I love.

I end up eating quickly and going back to my apartment to sulk. Once inside, I drop my bag with a heavy thunk and shrug off my coat.

I stand there in the middle of the floor for a minute, trying to summon the energy to do anything else. I turn back around and see the small piece of paper Lucas gave me lying on the floor. It must have fallen out of my coat.

I pick it up and stare at it for a moment, remembering the way he looked at me when he said, "Message me anytime." Maybe all Frenchmen naturally sound flirty, but maybe he was actually flirting with me.

What would be the harm in a quick message? I could take him up on his offer of a tour. I could simply thank him for being kind to me today. I could just say "hello."

My heart races just thinking about it. I picture him leaning over a table in some hidden Parisian bar, his eyes glinting in candlelight, his smile slow and sure. I picture that accent whispering my name in the dark.

We could have a tryst. It would be delicious. We would know it's just for my time here, and it means nothing more than two consenting adults enjoying each other's bodies. It would be so easy to give in to the urge.

I press the paper flat on my palm and close my eyes, picturing it. But instead of Lucas, I see the faces of four other men. My chest twists. What would they say about it? How would they feel if they knew I was daydreaming about another guy?

I let out a long, steadying breath. I'm not some ingenue flirting my way through Europe. I have four men back home who care about me and have generously agreed to this arrangement. They all care about me so much, I couldn't possibly add someone else into this complicated mix without at least talking to them about it first.

I put the paper away in a drawer and decide to try Melody instead. She needs me right now, and she never responded to my text. I'm starting to really worry about her.

It's early afternoon back home, so I hope I'm not interrupting her. When the phone rings twice, I'm almost sure she isn't going to answer. But she finally picks up on the third ring.

"Harper?"

Her voice is muffled. I hear rustling in the background, the faint whine of a baby.

"Hey," I say softly.

"Jesus, what time is it there?"

"It's eight," I tell her.

"Is everything okay?"

I smile sadly. She's deflecting. "Actually, I was calling to see if you're okay," I say carefully.

Melody is independent to a fault, so I don't want to spook her. If I show too much concern, she'll shut down.

She exhales. "Your mom called you, didn't she?" She sounds defeated more than anything else.

"She did," I confirm, knowing there's no use in beating around the bush. "She's worried about you, Mel."

"I know," she says, her voice breaking.

I hear her sniff, and I just wish I were there to comfort her. Despite everything she put me through in the past, I hate the idea of her dealing with all of this stress by herself.

"Mel, are you okay?"

She sighs heavily, and I hear another sniff. "I'm tired," she finally admits.

"Of course you are." I affirm her feelings sympathetically.

"No," she cuts me off. "I'm like… really tired. I can barely see straight. I'm not functioning very well."

I press my lips together.

"Are you thinking about hurting yourself?"

"No!" she says immediately, and I feel a little more at ease.

"That's good," I breathe. "I'm just worried about you, Mel. Promise me that you'll call me anytime if you need me. I will always answer, no matter what."

She's quiet for a moment before she finally answers with a small and broken, "Okay, I will."

1 2

———

THE VISITOR

Rafe

The second I step off the plane, my heart races like I'm about to walk into the biggest game of my life. I don't even care that I'm running on three hours of sleep and a terrible in-flight meal. I'm in Paris. I'm going to see Harper for the first time in weeks.

Even though we talk all the time, and I see her face every day on my phone screen, nothing compares to being in the same place. It's been so much harder than when I was in California.

The airport is loud and chaotic. People are moving in every direction, announcements are echoing loudly overhead, but all of that fades the second I spot her.

She's standing just past the gate, looking straight at me with a soft smile playing on her lips. Her hair's loose and a little wavy, tucked behind one ear, and she's wearing a pale blue sweater that makes her eyes look like the sky cracked open.

Paris suits her. She looks like she belongs here.

I don't even bother trying to play it cool. I drop my bag and take the last few steps to her in a rush, pulling her into my arms and holding her so tight she squeaks a little.

"Hi," she breathes, wrapping her arms around my neck. "You made it."

"Of course I made it," I murmur, kissing the side of her face, then her mouth, pulling back just enough to say, "I would never give up a chance to see you!"

She laughs against my lips. "I've missed you," she whispers.

"Yeah," I say, brushing my knuckles down her cheek. "Me, too."

We grab my bag, and she hails a cab like a pro. She's so confident here, speaking French like it's second nature, giving directions while I just sit back and stare at her, dazed and hungry and probably grinning like an idiot. The driver pulls up to a narrow building on a quiet street, and Harper guides me up three flights of stairs to her apartment.

The second the door closes behind us, I'm expecting a little tour or maybe some food. But she drops her keys on the counter, turns around, and walks straight up to me with a hungry look in her eyes. Before I can even ask what's going on, she reaches for my shirt and starts unbuttoning it with a quiet kind of intensity.

"Harper—" I start to say, but she shuts me up with a kiss.

It's not gentle. It's not slow. It's weeks of want and loneliness and heat packed into one kiss, and I don't know why I thought we'd ease into anything.

By the time my shirt hits the floor, my brain is already catching up. I slide my hands up her sides, feeling the soft knit of her sweater give way to skin underneath, and then I'm helping her strip out of her clothes, too. She pushes me back until the backs of my knees hit her bed, and I sit down hard, breathless.

"You sure?" I ask, my voice rough.

She nods without hesitation. "I've been waiting for this all week."

And that's all I need. I pull her down on top of me, and in a moment she's positioning herself above me, lining me up at her entrance. My head falls back as she lowers herself onto my cock, inch my inch, taking me in fully.

I'd forgotten how good it felt to be completely buried inside of her. I let her take the lead as she rides me, but I can't stop touching and kissing every inch of skin I can reach. She's a little tanner than when she left, but her skin is still just as smooth and soft. I pay special attention to the tits I've been deprived of for weeks. I'm mesmerized by the way they bounce as she rides me.

"Fuck, I've missed this," I groan as she starts riding me harder. "That's it. I'm moving to Paris!"

She giggles and kisses me, letting her tongue linger in my mouth until both of our breathing becomes too ragged. We breathe in the same air as we chase each other to our peak.

I can tell I'm closer to it than she is, so I slip my hand between us and apply a little pressure to her clit. Within seconds, she's coming undone around me, her walls squeezing me tight. I can't hold back anymore and spill inside of her.

We're a breathless, sweaty mess, and I think we just set a new record for our best time. When I tell her that, she throws her head back and laughs.

After we've cleaned up, we lay together in her bed. Her head is on my chest and she's drawing lazy circles on my skin.

"I didn't plan to jump you like that," she murmurs. "I just—"

"Don't apologize," I cut in breathlessly, tilting her face up to mine. "That was the best welcome I've ever gotten."

She smiles, her eyes soft. "I'm glad you're here."

I kiss her again, slower this time. "Me too."

When we finally pull ourselves away from each other, we spend the afternoon wandering through the streets of Paris lazily. She takes me to a bakery she loves, where we share a croissant that tastes better than any pastry I've ever had in my life. Then we hit a park where the trees are already turning gold. I bet fall here is absolutely insane. She shows me her school building from a distance and points out all her favorite hidden art murals on the sides of old buildings.

At one point, she stops in the middle of a cobblestone street and pulls me into a kiss. I don't even care that people are watching. I'm too wrapped up in her.

We walk along the Seine, and as we lean against the railing

looking out over the river, she nudges my side. "Can I ask you something?"

"Anything."

She takes a second, her fingers brushing mine. "Does it bother you?" she asks. "The media stuff, I mean?"

I turn toward her, confused.

"About you and Damien," she clarifies. "About me being with both of you. People are saying things."

I take a breath, looking her over carefully. There's something raw under her calm exterior, something uncertain she's trying to hide.

"I don't give a damn what they say," I tell her, plain and clear. "Let them talk. They don't know us."

"But it's not just gossip, Rafe. Apparently, this is headline-worthy. 'Bullet and Blackwood share mystery woman.' I saw that one this morning."

I reach for her hand and hold it tight. "You think I'm gonna let some internet noise get between us? You think I don't know who you are? What this is?" I shake my head. "I'm lucky to have you. Damien's lucky too. And anyone who doesn't get it can get fucked."

She exhales slowly, and I watch her shoulders relax. "Okay," she says quietly.

"I mean it," I tell her. "I don't care if the whole world is watching. Let them be confused. Let them be mad. I've got nothing to prove to anyone but you."

* * *

HARPER

Paris becomes so much more romantic with Rafe here. My loneliness evaporates with him beside me, holding my hand as we walk down the streets, and staring at me longingly over breakfast.

We've spent the whole day wandering without much of a plan. We stopped at a flower market, where he bought me a single sunflower that's now sticking out of my bag. Then, we ducked into a tiny gallery filled with abstract pieces that reminded me of the first time I ever let him see one of my paintings. After that, we found a bookstore where he read the English titles out loud in a fake French accent, making me snort-laugh so hard I startled a cat curled up by the window.

Now we sit across from each other at a quiet little bistro near the Eiffel Tower. The candles flicker low on the table between us, casting shadows on his face that make his jaw look even sharper than usual. He has on one of his favorite blue shirts, and I can't stop staring at how it brings out his eyes.

He catches me looking and smirks. "Like what you see, Ward?"

I smile and pop the last bite of my duck into my mouth. "You're not terrible to look at," I shrug playfully.

His eyes glint, playful and just the right amount of suggestive. He leans forward, resting his elbow on the table. He lowers his voice so only I can hear. *"Voulez-vous coucher avec moi?"*

I burst out laughing, so loud that the couple next to us glances over at us curiously. "Oh, my god," I gasp, trying to catch my breath. "That's my line."

He chuckles smugly. "Well, you've been hogging all the French. I figured I'd try the only phrase I know."

I shake my head, wiping the corner of my mouth with a napkin. "It's my bedroom we'll be sleeping in," I tease. "So maybe I should be the only one asking."

"At least you know I'm ready and willing," he says, his eyes twinkling in the candlelight.

I glance around for our waiter. "," I say when I catch his eye.

Rafe raises an eyebrow. "What did you just say?"

"I asked for the check."

"So that's a yes?" he asks with a wolfish grin.

I reach across the table and slide my fingers into his. "That's a 'hell yes!"

The second the door closes behind us at my apartment, the air changes. He backs me into the wall before I can take off my coat, his hands slipping under the hem and pushing it off my shoulders. My breath catches when his lips find that spot just below my ear, the one that makes my knees wobble.

"If I haven't said it enough, I've fucking missed you," he murmurs against my skin.

"Maybe just once more," I breathe, tugging at his shirt.

Clothes drop in record speed across the floor as we stumble our way to the bed. Every movement is familiar and urgent, since we're trying to make up for lost time. His mouth is hot on mine, his hands firm and reverent as they move across my body.

He gently guides me to a lying position on the bed and settles between my open legs. I gasp as he pushes open my entrance with his tongue. My whole body trembles as he enters me with three fingers and makes circles on my clit with his tongue. My body is a canvas, and he's a very skilled painter.

"Fuck, baby," I whine. "I need more."

"Your wish is my command," he says, leaving one last lingering kiss at my entrance.

He climbs on top of me and slams inside, a little rougher than I'm used to from him, but I love it. I urge him on to a sloppy, punishing pace that leaves us both breathing raggedly and screaming out at the top of my lungs.

I know my neighbors probably hate me by now. This is the fourth time we've done this since he arrived yesterday, and that's nothing compared to how loud Damien made me holler when he visited.

Afterward, tangled in sheets and sweat, I lie with my head on his chest, making imaginary patterns on his ribs with my fingers.

"So I think one of my co-workers is flirting with me," I say softly.

His fingers still, but only for a second. "Oh?"

I lift my head to look at him. "He offered to give me a tour of the city. And he gave me his IG. He told me to message him any time, and I swear he winked when he said it."

He nods slowly, smirking at me. "Is he cute?"

I laugh once. "He's gorgeous."

"Honest. I like it."

I rest my chin on his chest. "Would it bother you if I went on a tour with him? Just as friends, I mean."

He studies my face for a moment, then smooths his hand down my back. "No," he says. "It wouldn't bother me. You're a strong woman, Harper. You can handle yourself anywhere and with anyone. You proved that with Jeff."

Ah, Jeff McNaught–his misogynistic ex-teammate who basically tried to assault me. I handed him his ass, though. And if Lucas tries to get fresh with me, I can do the same.

"You should go," he adds. "Let the guy take you out and have fun. Just be careful. Trust your instincts."

I nod again, slower this time. "I will."

"You deserve it," he says.

1 3

INSTA-STALKING

My students chatter to each other in French, their voices overlapping as they work. It's only been a few weeks, but I'm finally starting to get into the rhythm of teaching.

I don't feel like a total imposter anymore at least. Just a tiny one. Most days, I still can't believe this is my life.

My students are absolutely brilliant. Scarily so, in some cases. One of them, Léa, is a master at sketching. Painting isn't her medium, but even so, she's taken to it with the same precision she uses in her drawings.

Another, a boy named Jules, specializes in sculpting. Last week, he showed me one of his busts, and it was so lifelike, I was sure it was going to start talking to me.

And they're sweet, too, which is a nice bonus. They have a million questions for me about what America is like, and they're always eager to give me recommendations for places to go here in Paris. Yesterday, one of the students brought me macarons from a place near the Seine that apparently has the best rosewater flavor in the entire city. They were good, but I'll still stick with pistachio.

And it's not just school that's making me feel welcome. The city itself is a living, breathing work of art. Even on the most ordinary of days, I find things that surprise me. I'll turn a corner and find myself in front of a mural I've never noticed, or a bakery I swear wasn't there the day before.

I try new pastries every day. I've developed a real thing for *pain au chocolat,* and I already know this will be the hardest thing to give up when I'm back in Minnesota. Some nights, I walk home along the cobblestone streets, a little tipsy from a glass of red wine, with the Eiffel Tower glowing in the distance, and I just want to cry from how lucky I am.

Despite all of that, I still miss my guys. I miss Damien's extravagant way of showing me affection. I miss the comfort of just being around Rafe. I miss spending a day on Scott's farm, and taking a literal roll in the hay when we're already sweaty and exhausted. I miss dancing with Tomas, and hearing his warm, passionate Spanish.

God, I miss Tomás so much it actually aches sometimes. He and Scott are the two I haven't seen in the longest–my sweet, grounded farmer and my thoughtful, poetry-loving professor. It doesn't feel right without them. I find myself reaching for my phone to text them, only to remember that they're probably asleep or in the middle of something. The time difference is still a bitch.

It also doesn't help that I keep finding myself daydreaming about my handsome co-worker. Even though Rafe said he'd be okay with me going on a tour with him, I haven't told him how attracted I am to Lucas. And I haven't talked to the others about him at all. He's a delicious secret, but I can't stop the guilt that blooms in my stomach whenever I think about him.

It's late by the time I get home after my class. My boots click softly against the marble stairs of my apartment building. I've been on my feet all day, and my brain is still buzzing from critiques and lesson planning. I kick off my shoes the second I step inside and pour myself a generous glass of wine, then curl up on my couch in an oversized sweatshirt and leggings. The city hums quietly outside my window.

I scroll through my phone without really seeing anything. My

Instagram feed is full of art, fashion, and the occasional travel blogger, all set against golden light and beautiful streets that, for once, actually resemble the world outside my own window. I should be content. And I am. Mostly.

But then I pause. My gaze flicks toward the tiny drawer in my desk with guilty fascination. The slip of paper is still there, tucked beside a stray pencil and a half-used tube of lip balm. I pull it out slowly, unfolding it slowly like it might bite me.

His Instagram handle is scrawled in sharp black ink. I stare at it for a few long seconds before letting out a breath and opening the search bar.

"A little Insta-stalking won't hurt anything," I mumble to myself.

The screen loads, and I blink at the header. His profile picture is a black-and-white photo of him with a sculpture in the background. His username is just his name. His bio just says: *Sculpteur. Paris. Matière et émotion*: Sculptor. Paris. Material and emotion.

He's perfectly mastered the vague and sexy artist aesthetic.

I start scrolling through his profile and I'm immediately hooked.

His sculptures are stunning. They're raw and textured and full of movement. There are close-ups of rough stone, smooth marble, and soft clay, all shaped by hands that clearly know what they're doing. One piece shows a figure curled in on itself, its arms wrapped tight around its knees. There's so much detail in the shoulder blades, tension in the way the fingers dig into the flesh. Every inch of it is breathtaking.

Another shows a bust of a woman with her head tilted back, her lips parted like she's mid-breath. It's sensual without being overtly so, and effortlessly expressive.

Photos of his art are interspersed with photos of him working in his studio, his shirt pushed up to his elbows, curls falling over his forehead, and smudges of clay on his hands. In one photo, he's concentrating so hard his eyebrows furrow, his lips slightly parted. In another, he's laughing with someone off-camera, joy lighting up his whole face.

I pause on that one, just looking. I've tried so hard not to think about how stunning he is.

I've caught glimpses of him in the hallway. His studio's not far from mine, and sometimes we cross paths during breaks or as we're leaving for the day. Every time, he looks ridiculously good. Besides his obvious physical attributes, there's also an ease about him that makes everything he does look deliberate and unhurried. He always has some kind of notebook or sketchpad in hand. He always looks relaxed and just one word away from bursting out in happy laughter.

As I look at his photos, I finally let myself feel the curiosity and attraction that I've kept buried down in his presence. Here, in the privacy of my home, there's no harm in letting myself give into the fantasy of him.

How could anything be sexier than a French sculptor?

I swipe through another few more posts. There's a video of him shaping clay, his hands moving in practiced circles, the camera focused on the spinning form. His voice floats in from offscreen, soft and low, explaining something about symmetry and texture in French. It sends a shiver down my spine.

I shift on the couch, suddenly warm. My wine glass is nearly empty, and I can't tell if it's the alcohol or the man on my screen making my heart race.

I don't let myself message him. That would be a step too far. Insta-stalking is one thing, but actually engaging is a whole other line I'm not willing to cross. It's just appreciation, I tell myself. Artistic admiration. It doesn't mean anything.

But the image of him lingers anyway, like a half-finished sculpture in my mind.

I shake my head, already annoyed with myself for getting so wrapped up in one Instagram feed. It's nothing, just a little harmless scrolling. Everyone does it. Still, I know myself well enough to know when I'm on the edge of a slippery slope.

The best thing I can do right now is distract myself. And since it's been one of those long, paint-splattered, coffee-stained, lovely-but-exhausting days, I decide to run a bath.

The small bathroom fills with steam while I move around my apartment, pulling my hair into a messy knot and lighting a few lavender-scented candles.

I sink into the warm water and exhale until my shoulders drop. I stay there for a while, soaking in silence, trying not to think about anything or anyone, but it's a useless effort. Thoughts of Lucas sneak in anyway, and I try not to let my mind wander farther than just surface attraction. Because I could really get carried away if I don't control it.

I don't let myself stay in the bath long. It's too easy to get dreamy in the tub, and I know that where those daydreams will lead. The cold air on my skin when I get out is enough to shock my senses so I can think more clearly.

Once I'm dry and in my favorite sleep shirt, one that I stole from Rafe years ago, I towel off my hair and flop onto the bed. My body is still warm and pleasantly heavy from the bath. I reach for my phone without thinking, and when the screen lights up, I freeze.

There's a notification.

New message from: lucas_moreau

Oh, no. I blink at the screen, my heart picking up speed as I open the app. The notification pulls me into my messages, and right there at the top is a message from Lucas.

Bonsoir, chérie.

That's it. Two words. But my stomach flutters like he sent a love letter. I immediately sit up straighter in bed, suddenly wide awake. I scroll up just to make sure I'm not missing something, and that's when I realize, to my horror, that I accidentally liked one of his older photos. It's a shot of a wire-and-glass installation hanging from the ceiling of a gallery, thankfully, and not one of him, but it's still over a year old.

Apparently, when I tossed my phone earlier, I'd smacked the screen hard enough to tap "like" on one of his posts. I groan softly into my hands. This is such a classic Harper move. I didn't mean to actually engage him. Now he knows I was looking. More than looking, he knows I was digging through his feed.

I go back to his message. *Bonsoir chérie.*

He probably doesn't mean anything by it. French is naturally flirtatious, right? It doesn't have to mean anything. Still, I stare at the message for a long time before finally tapping out a reply. I have to play this just right.

Bonsoir, Lucas. That installation is beautiful. I love the way you used negative space.

I hit send before I can overthink it. This is good. I just have to keep it focused and about his art. Otherwise, I risk it turning into something else. A minute later, his reply comes through.

Merci. It was a difficult piece, but I'm glad it speaks to you. I admire your work too. That piece in the staff lounge with the cityscape—c'est magnifique.

I smile, lowering the phone for a second. I only brought in a small canvas for the lounge last week, something I painted during the first few days in Paris when I couldn't sleep. I didn't even think anyone had noticed it.

Thank you. I painted that during my first week here. Everything felt so new, I just wanted to get the feeling down before it faded.

He replies within seconds.

It hasn't faded, has it? I like the way your eyes light up when you talk about Paris.

Now I don't know what to say. That feels flirtier than the rest, but still subtle enough to ignore if I want to. Do I want to? I type and delete a few versions of my reply before finally settling on something neutral.

It's hard not to fall in love with Paris. It's all color and motion and light. The whole city feels like a living canvas.

I send it and then immediately tuck the phone under my pillow, hoping that'll keep me from saying anything else tonight. I'm not crossing any lines. We're just a couple of artists appreciating each other's work. This is nothing more than friendly, professional admiration.

I pull the covers over my legs and turn off the lamp, staring at the ceiling in the darkness. But even after the light's out and the city quiets around me, I can't stop smiling.

Lucas noticed my work.

Lucas messaged me first.

Lucas called me chérie.

The word hums through me like a low chord of music I wasn't expecting.

Tomorrow, I'll see him at work. We'll pass in the hallway or nod in the break room, and maybe this little exchange will fade into nothing. Maybe it'll be something we don't even mention. Just a small, fluttering moment between two artists in Paris.

Or maybe it'll be something else entirely.

14

AN ENTICING INVITATION

The afternoon sunlight filters through the tall windows of the staff break room, casting a soft golden glow over the whole room. Lucas is leaning against the counter near the espresso machine, one hand curled around a tiny porcelain cup of strong black coffee, the other tucked casually into his slacks. He's mid-sentence, laughing about something one of his students said during class, and I can't help but smile.

I'm standing across from him, stirring a little sugar into my own coffee, half listening, half admiring how he's always so effortlessly put together. Today he's wearing a crisp blue button-down shirt with the sleeves rolled up to his elbows. A few of his curls fall across his forehead, and he makes no motion to push them away. He's so easy, so comfortable in his own skin, but I have to keep my guard up around him.

Across the room, a few of the other teachers are chatting near the fruit bowl, and our boss, Andre, is perched on a stool with a thick folder in his lap, flipping through papers. That's why I'm caught off guard when Lucas glances up at me between sips and says, "Harper, have you ever been to the Théâtre de l'Atelier?"

I look up at him in surprise.

"No," I answer shyly. "I haven't really had a chance to visit any of the theaters here."

"There's a play this weekend," he says. "A modern interpretation of Cyrano. I think you might enjoy it. Would you like to come with me?"

The words hang there for a second, and I can feel eyes shifting subtly in our direction. Then again, maybe it's just my insecurity. I always feel like I'm on display no matter where I am.

I tuck a piece of hair behind my ear and nod quickly.

"Sure," I answer casually. "That sounds fun. I'll be able to cross that off my Paris bucket list."

Lucas smiles, and it's that slow, warm grin that makes something flutter in my stomach. "Perfect. I'll text you the details later."

He doesn't linger after. He nods and takes his coffee over to the couch, where he sits with a few of the other teachers. I stand there for a moment longer, staring down into my mug, feeling oddly flushed.

It didn't feel like he was asking me on a date. Not with everyone in the room. Not with how casually he said it. But still, there's a buzz beneath my skin. I can't tell if it's excitement or nerves or guilt, but I definitely feel flustered. I decide to finish my coffee in my classroom, because being around all these people makes me want to combust.

LATER THAT EVENING, AFTER A HOT SHOWER AND A QUICK DINNER, I curl up on the couch in my apartment with my phone pressed to my ear and a glass of wine in my hand.

"He asked you to a play?" Damien's voice is amused on the other end of the line. "Are French men always this smooth, or is it just the ones you work with?"

I laugh, curling my legs beneath me. "It wasn't like that. He asked me in front of everyone. Andre was right there. It felt more like a friendly offer than anything else."

"Still," Damien says, "he clearly wants to spend time with you."

"We work together," I reply, swirling the wine in my glass. "And it's a play. It's not like he invited me to a candlelit dinner."

"Mm," Damien hums. "And if he had?"

"Then I would have said no."

There's a pause. "Would you?"

"Yes," I say firmly, setting my wine down. "I'm not looking for something new. I already have four amazing men who make my life complicated and beautiful enough."

His chuckle is warm. "But you could if you wanted to, you know."

I exhale slowly, letting my head fall back against the cushions. "Even if it was a date, I'm not interested. I like him, but not like that."

There's another pause, and I can tell Damien is really measuring out what he wants to say. "I trust you, Harper," he finally says. "You don't have to explain yourself to me."

My heartstrings pull at that. "I know. I just wanted you to hear it from me first, before I end up in some random tabloid with a photo of us walking into the theater together."

He laughs again, the sound so bright and happy. "We really do need to get you a better coat and sunglasses if you're going to keep becoming internet famous."

I groan, remembering the most recent headline I saw about me. "Or I could just stay in my apartment and paint forever. Then they'd forget I exist altogether."

"That does sound like a great way to avoid the press," Damien says, then adds in a lower voice, "But it's a little selfish on your part. Because I wouldn't get to see you either."

"You can see me whenever you want," I remind him. "And you have a private jet and a private villa. We could spend plenty of time together without ever going out in public."

"True," he chuckles. "But I like showing you off."

His tone becomes possessive, and I can't help but think of all those gallery openings he's taken me to, with his arm wrapped firmly around my waist.

"It would be a shame to stay cooped up in the house all the time," I answer absent-mindedly. Sometimes, the most fun Damien and I have is in the public foreplay before we're able to enjoy each other in private.

"You're going to have an amazing time," Damien says, cutting through my lustful thoughts. "Theatre in Paris is unlike anywhere else in the world. It'll ruin you for theatre anywhere else."

I smile into the phone, tucking my feet beneath me as I lean back against the armrest of the couch. "I don't have much experience with theatre in general," I remind him.

"Well, we'll have to fix that right away," he says, and I can hear the amusement in his voice. "We'll do a week in New York sometime, and I'll take you to every production we can get into."

A warm flush runs through me. I grip the phone tighter. "That's sweet."

"I can't let my girl stay so horribly uncultured," he jokes.

There's a pause, and I can hear the faint rustle of fabric on his end, like he's settled into something plush. Probably his over-the-top velvet armchair in that penthouse he barely uses. I picture him with a whiskey in hand, his legs crossed, his eyes glinting as he speaks.

"And I'm glad," he continues, "that you've made a new friend. It means you're not just locked in your apartment waiting for us to visit… that you're living."

"That's what this is all about, right?" I say softly. "A new life, a new chapter. Paris was supposed to wake something in me."

"And has it?" His voice lowers.

I think about it for a second. I've settled into a new routine here, but it's still miles different from anything I did at home. I've really had to push myself out of my comfort zone. "Yeah," I say. "It really has."

"Good," he murmurs. "Then maybe I can take credit for being part of that transformation."

I laugh under my breath. "You definitely can."

There's a beat of silence before he continues, "Besides, if it weren't for me, you probably wouldn't be an international scandal."

"Oh, God," I groan, dropping my head back onto the cushion. "Don't remind me."

"Has your mom given you any more grief about your heartbreaker status?" he asks, clearly enjoying himself.

"We've agreed that my love life is completely off-limits."

He chuckles. "The poor woman probably thinks you've joined a cult."

"I think she'd prefer that to 'the mystery woman who's seducing athletes and billionaires alike.'"

"Seduce is such a harsh word," Damien says, his voice silken. "I prefer 'enchanted.' You enchanted us."

I cover my face with one hand. "Please stop."

"But I'm serious," he says. "You've become an online obsession–Reddit threads, gossip blogs, tabloid Instagram accounts. I even saw one article speculating that you're some kind of elite heiress who's been hiding in plain sight."

I snort. "I don't know whether to laugh or cry."

"Laugh," Damien says immediately. "Always laugh about it. I don't like it when you cry."

"I haven't yet," I joke, but I can't pretend that it hasn't been getting to me.

Damien's voice softens. "Does all this negative attention bother you?"

I consider the question before answering with something flippant like I usually do. "I think it bothers me that people are talking about me like I'm not real. Like I'm just some Midwest floozy with no morals. They don't see the full picture. They don't see us."

"I see you," he says thoughtfully, and I can't help but melt a little.

"Do you regret it?" I ask, quieter now. "Being seen with me like that?"

He exhales, and when he speaks, there's not a single ounce of hesitation in his tone. "I get to kiss the most beautiful woman in the world as the world watches enviously. Why would that bother me?"

"Damien," I chastise.

"I mean it," he adds. "How does that saying go? If kissing you in front of the world is wrong, I don't want to be right."

I can't help but laugh at that, and still I know that there's so much truth behind his words. He cares about me far more than he cares about anyone's opinion, and that means the world.

"Thank you," I say finally. "That means more than you know."

"I hope you'll think of me when you're watching that play," he says, his voice shifting again, teasing. "Pretend I'm the one sitting beside you."

I smile. "Only if you send snacks."

"No promises."

We hang up, and I'm still staring at the phone when there's a knock at the door.

Curious, I pad over and open it. A teenage boy in a black jacket stands on the other side holding a rectangular box wrapped in matte black paper.

"Pour Harper?" he asks, his voice thick with an accent.

"Oui, that's me," I say, surprised.

He nods, hands me the box with a quick smile, and disappears down the hallway before I can even ask who sent it. I close the door behind me, locking it, and carry the box to the kitchen counter. There's no card. No label. Just the sleekest wrapping I've ever seen. I pull the ribbon loose and peel back the lid.

The dress inside makes me gasp. It's deep navy blue, with delicate beadwork across the bodice and a soft drape that catches the light as I shift it around. It's elegant, timeless, but somehow modern. I've never seen anything so beautiful, and I've certainly never worn anything this amazing, even considering some of the more extravagant dresses Damien has sent.

And then, of course, I realize that he's done it again. He's spoiled me with couture, and he isn't even going to be the one reaping the benefits of it.

I hold it up in front of me and spin slightly, grinning.

"How does Damien do that?" I mutter, laughing softly to myself.

15

———

AN UNPLEASANT ENCOUNTER

I haven't been to a play since before college, so seeing one in Paris is even more exciting. As soon as the lights go dim and the velvet curtain rises, a hush falls over the crowd and an exciting energy shoots through me. I sit beside Lucas, our knees almost touching, and let myself get swept up in the warm murmur of French conversation that surrounds us.

The actors are brilliant, even if I only catch half of what's being said. I understand just enough to follow the plot, but it's the sets and fabulous makeup that really pull me in. Lucas occasionally leans in to whisper a word or phrase to help me keep up, and the way his breath brushes my ear sends tiny shivers over my skin. But it's not flirtatious, I keep reminding myself. This is just friendly.

When the play ends, we step out into the chilled night air, the golden glow of street lamps dancing across wet cobblestones. I expect Lucas to say goodnight then, but instead he gestures toward a nearby alley.

"There is a little place I love," he says. "Only if you're not too tired?"

"I'm never too tired for a drink," I reply with a grin, and he offers his arm like an old-fashioned gentleman.

The bar is tucked down a narrow side street, nearly invisible from the main road. Inside, it's dimly lit and charmingly cluttered with mismatched chairs, flickering candles, and dusty bottles stacked behind the bar. We find a table near the back, and I sink into a well-worn armchair while Lucas orders for us. Two glasses of red wine appear moments later, and we clink them together with a soft, "*Santé.*"

"This place is perfect," I say, looking around.

He smiles at me, his eyes glowing in the soft lighting.

"This is one of my favorite spots," he smirks. "Tourists usually can't find it."

"I like that," I admit. "It makes me feel like I belong here."

"Maybe you do belong here," he murmurs.

I can't stop the blush that creeps up my cheeks.

We talk about art for a while, about his sculptures, my paintings, and the things that inspire us. He tells me about his favorite gallery tucked near the Seine, and I tell him about the high school art teacher who inspired me to start painting. There are no awkward pauses or jittery butterflies. We really are just two colleagues out on the town. Nothing more.

When we finally leave, it's late. We walk side by side, his hands in his coat pockets, mine tucked into my sleeves.

"Thank you for tonight," I say as we approach my building. "It was nice to do something other than getting wine drunk in my apartment."

He stops just outside my door and turns to face me with a boyish smirk.

"It was a pleasure, Harper. Truly."

There's a pause, just a flicker too long, where I think maybe he'll try and kiss me. And maybe I want him to. But instead, Lucas reaches for my hand, lifts it to his lips, and presses the faintest kiss to my knuckles.

Then he backs away down the street and calls out, *"J'ai le béguin!"*

He's smitten.

The words echo off the stone walls, and I can't help but laugh. I blush so hard my cheeks sting, standing there grinning like an idiot as he disappears around the corner.

It takes me a full ten minutes to go inside.

The next few days pass quietly. At school, Lucas and I are nothing but professional. A nod in the hall. A smile in the break room. Nothing inappropriate or lingering. It's almost as if the night never happened at all, which is both a relief and a disappointment.

I throw myself into my classes. My students are thriving. There's one girl in particular who's started staying after class to get my help with her shading and light. I let her linger as long as she wants. Watching her blossom under the smallest bit of encouragement is one of the most fulfilling things I've ever experienced as both an artist and a teacher.

The school is really starting to feel like my home away from home. I've learned which vending machine always eats your coins, which coffee pot to avoid, and which hallway smells weird after it rains. I've figured out that Mondays are the hardest and Fridays are the fastest, and that the sculpting wing stays warm long after the rest of the building goes cold.

It's Thursday when Andre corners me in the break room.

"Miss Ward," he says in that smooth, slightly amused voice of his. "Do you have a moment before you leave this afternoon?"

I pause, cup of coffee halfway to my lips.

"Of course," I tell him, suddenly feeling nervous for no discernible reason. "Is everything okay?"

"Everything is great," he replies. "Just stop by my office. It won't take very long."

He walks off before I can ask anything else, and I spend the rest of the day with nervous butterflies in my stomach. I replay the last few weeks in my head, trying to make sure I haven't inadvertently done something wrong.

By the time the day is over, I'm sweating. I make my way to his office, my boots echoing down the empty hall. I pause outside his door, take a deep breath, and knock.

"Entrez," he calls.

I step inside nervously. He gestures to one of the chairs across from him, and I sit down, heart hammering.

He smiles warmly.

"Relax, Harper. You're not in trouble."

I finally let myself take a relaxing breath.

"Oh, good," I say with a quick laugh.

"In fact, quite the opposite," he continues. "I wanted to tell you how pleased we are with your work."

My shoulders drop, and I smile.

"Thank you. That means a lot."

"You bring something fresh to the school," he says. "Your passion, your technique, the way you speak to the students, it's all been very well received."

I feel my cheeks flush.

"I've really enjoyed it here. The students are incredible."

Andre leans back in his chair.

"I agree. And we are so happy with your work, I hope you'll consider staying for the second semester."

Another wave of peace crashes over me, and I can't help but feel a little pleased, though truthfully I haven't decided if I'm going to stay or not.

"We'd be lucky to have you," he says, as if he's reading my mind. "I know you originally committed to one term, but you've made a real impression."

I nod at his encouragement and accept his compliments with the practiced modesty I've learned as a struggling artist.

But then, something shifts.

It's subtle at first. The way his voice drops, just slightly, as he compliments not my work but about me. The way his eyes linger a second longer than they should when he mentions how refreshing it is to have someone "so young and vibrant" on staff. The way his smile seems less warm and more appraising.

I try to brush it off. Maybe it's cultural. Maybe it's nothing. But then, Andre pushes back from his desk. I don't move. I assume he's going to grab something off the shelf or check his calendar, but instead, he circles around his desk slowly, until he's behind me.

My whole body stiffens.

And then, without asking, without warning, his hands settle on my shoulders. His thumbs press lightly into the space between my neck and my collarbone, and he begins to massage.

"You really are special, Harper," he says, voice low and smooth. "Not just as an artist, but as a woman, too."

I freeze. For a second, I don't know what to do. My body locks up, my brain lagging behind what's happening. It's not forceful. He's not grabbing me. But that somehow his casual intimacy makes the moment so much worse. It's almost like he thinks he's earned this, like I should be grateful that he's blessed me with his affection.

I find my voice. It's quiet and not as forceful as I would like, but at least I'm able to form words.

"Please don't touch me like that," I say, standing abruptly. His hands fall away, and I turn to face him, heart pounding so hard I feel it in my ears. "You don't have my consent to touch me like that."

Andre tilts his head, clearly surprised, but not apologetic.

"Pardon me," he begins, then chuckles. "I assumed it was fine."

Embarrassment washes over me. But why should I feel embarrassed? He's the one who's crossed a boundary!

"Why would you think that?" I ask with venom in my voice.

He shrugs one shoulder, expression far too calm for what he just did.

"Well, you're sleeping with Rafe Maloney and Damien Blackwood, aren't you? And I've heard that now you're dating our own Lucas. I thought you were open to this."

His words are like a sharp slap across my face. My jaw clenches, and my eyes feel with tears that I refuse to shed in front of him.

"Excuse me?" I ask with every ounce of anger I can muster.

Andre steps forward, holding his hands up like he's trying to appear harmless, but I see the arrogance underneath. "Come now, Harper. You're clearly passionate. I thought maybe—" He places his hands on my shoulders and brings his face closer to mine, like he's about to kiss me. I shove him back hard.

He stumbles a step, and his eyes flash with surprise, but I'm already halfway to the door.

"Don't you ever touch me again," I snap, my voice shaking now, tears burning behind my eyes. "Don't you ever talk to me like that again."

"Harper—" he starts, an argument already on his tongue, but I don't give him the chance to finish.

I slam the door behind me, heart racing, legs moving on pure instinct as I barrel down the hall.

I barely make it outside before the tears fall.

I don't stop walking. I don't look back. The October air is crisp, biting against my damp cheeks. My hands are trembling, and I clench my fists so tightly, my nails dig into my palms. I try to put as much space between myself and the school as possible.

It takes me exactly twelve minutes to get back to my apartment. I slam the door behind me, lock it, and toss my bag onto the floor before crumbling against the wall. My shoulders shake. I bury my face in my hands and let it all come out. All the rage and the shame and confusion tangled together in a sick knot inside my chest.

How dare he?

I'm not even sure how long I sit there before I finally pull out my phone. My hands still tremble as I unlock the screen, and I don't hesitate. I don't need to think. I don't need time to process. I need to get the hell out of here.

I find Damien's name, hit the button, and press the phone to my ear.

He picks up after the first ring.

"Harper? What's going on?"

The concern in his voice undoes me all over again. I break out into another round of tears, and he waits patiently for me to speak. Finally, I manage to tell him what happened, and I can hear the fury behind his voice.

"I'll kill him," he says quietly, dangerously.

"I don't know what to do," I whisper. "I love teaching. I love my students. He violated me and made me feel small."

"You're not small," Damien says, voice kinder. "You're incredible. You didn't deserve that. And you sure as hell don't have to stay somewhere that makes you feel unsafe."

I close my eyes and lean my head against my door.

"Should I come home?"

He doesn't answer right away, but I know it's not because he wants me to. He doesn't want to say the wrong thing, and I love him for that.

"I want you to be comfortable," he says. "And if you aren't comfortable there, then you should come back. You don't owe anyone your time. Not him. Not that school. If you want to stay, we'll figure it out. I'll make some calls and find you a better program."

My throat tightens.

"I just miss you guys so much," I admit, feeling pathetic.

"I know," he says gently. "And we miss you too."

"I really thought I could do this," I whisper meekly.

"You have done it," he says fiercely. "And you've been incredible. You've made a life for yourself in a new country. You've taught and inspired your students. But you don't have to prove anything to anyone, Harper. Especially not to that bastard."

I wipe my eyes, taking a deep breath.

"Will you come get me?"

His answer is immediate.

"I'm already on my way."

16

COMING HOME

DAMIEN

When the plane touches down in Paris, it's early morning. Fog clings to the runway, and the city is still half-asleep. I head straight for her apartment, and she's waiting by the door when I arrive, her packed suitcases at her side.

The second she sees me, she rushes forward, and I catch her mid-step, my arms winding tight around her waist. Her face buries into my chest, and I feel her sigh, all that tension easing just a little as I hold her close.

"Hi," she murmurs.

"Hi," I say back, kissing the top of her head. "Let's get you out of here."

We don't talk much on the way to the airport. She curls into me on the plane, her fingers laced with mine, her head resting against my shoulder. I let her sleep while I make a few quiet calls. I want Andre gone. I want every trace of him scrubbed from that school. I want his career burned to the ground.

I call in a favor with a friend who sits on the board of directors. By the time we hit cruising altitude, I've sent him a copy of Harper's

115

written statement and let him know in no uncertain terms that if Andre is still employed by the end of the day, I'll make sure every donor in the country knows that the school protects predators. And I'll make sure they see receipts.

They call me back before we even land. Andre's been dismissed. Effective immediately.

When Harper wakes up, she gives me a small smile, and I brush a piece of hair out of her eyes.

"He's gone," I tell her softly. "I had him dismissed. Permanently."

She looks slightly relieved, but she also looks dejected somehow. "Good," she says. "He doesn't deserve to be anywhere near a classroom."

I can't argue with that.

"If you want to press charges, or go public with this, I'll do whatever I can to support you."

She shakes her head slowly. "I just want to go home," she answers in a small voice.

The flight is fast after that. We talk a little, about inane topics. She asks about my work, and then asks me to catch her up on the others. I fill her in on Rafe's game schedule and how Scott's harvest is going. Tomas has been buried in his classes this semester, so I don't know much about what he's been doing the last few months. She smiles and listens, but I see the rage underneath her smile.

And honestly, I'm glad.

Harper isn't broken. She's not shrinking or hiding or doubting her worth. She's pissed, hurt, and furious. That fire in her eyes tells me she's going to be just fine.

When we step off the jet in Minnesota, she takes a deep, calming breath.

"Smells like home," she mutters sarcastically under her breath.

I chuckle. "Welcome back."

She smiles, but it doesn't quite reach her eyes. I take her suitcase and lead her toward the car.

Once we're in the backseat, she looks out the window for a few minutes, watching the fields blur past. I let her be, just listening to the soft hum of the tires on the road, until she finally turns toward me.

"Thank you," she says quietly. "For getting me out of there."

"You don't have to thank me for that," I tell her earnestly.

She reaches over, placing her hand on my thigh. "Still. It means a lot."

I cover her hand with mine. "How are you feeling?"

She contemplates this for a moment, choosing her words carefully. "I'm feeling a lot of things," she finally answers. "I'm so happy that I got to experience Paris so thoroughly. It wasn't just a tourist-y vacation, I felt like between you, Rafe, and Lucas, I really got to see the real Paris."

I nod. "That's good," I murmur, glad that she at least had that.

"Yeah. I mean, it was a great experience until it wasn't, you know." She looks out the window again, her eyes distant but thoughtful. "Teaching was great, and eating food in Paris was great. Drinking wine in the shadow of the Eiffel Tower was great." She smiles a little, but then her expression becomes more somber. "So, I'm really sad that it had to end so abruptly. And I'm sad for how it ended. I'm sad that Tomas and Scott didn't have a chance to come visit me there. And I'm so pissed at Andre, I could scream."

"But you're glad that you did it?" I can't help but asking.

She nods. "As weird as it may sound, I think I'd do it all again, even knowing how it would end. But for now, I'm just going to focus on the good things. It really is nice being back home."

We pull up to my apartment building a few minutes later. McKenzie doesn't know she's home yet, and Harper is too tired to deal with it tonight, which I don't blame her for. Here, she can rest and recuperate before she faces the world again.

"I think I'm going to sleep for a week," she sighs when we step off the elevator into my penthouse.

I smile. "I have the guest room all made up for you," I say, even though I know she isn't going to be spending any time in there.

"The guest room?" she asks, wrinkling her nose, and I can't help but chuckle at her disgust. "Are you sick of me already?"

"I could never be sick of you, little red bird," I murmur, pulling her into an embrace.

She wraps her arms around my neck and reaches up on her tiptoes to kiss me. We stand there for a moment, just feeling each other again. She was so upset on the plane, so I didn't push her, and even now I want her to take lead. After what that asshole put her through, I refuse to do anything to make her feel uncomfortable.

"Well," she finally says when we break away. "That's good, because I do have a few things I'd like to do before I crash."

She grabs my hand and leads me to my bedroom.

* * *

HARPER

"Fuck, Damien," I scream, as he pounds into me with all the force of a man who's missed me for two months. "I'm not going to last."

"Let it last a little longer and you'll love it more," he growls, which only increases my excitement.

We're sweaty and panting, and I really can't hold out much longer with the way he's taking me from behind and circling my clit with his thumb. I'm leaning over the bed with one leg perched on top, and this position is insane. I'm so far gone, I'm barely able to keep myself up.

"Please," I whine, and I don't even care that I'm begging for it.

He pats me on the ass lightly, and I can't help but roll my hips further into his fingers. Fuck, I'm really hanging on by the thinnest thread.

"You're so good, little red bird," he moans.

Our weeks apart have done nothing to lessen the effects that voice has on me. I scream out his name, trying to get some form of release before my body shatters. I'm clawing out of my skin, so desperate to come undone.

He pumps into me quicker, his fingers circling my clit at a punishing speed, and I'm about to weep when he finally says, "Now you can get there. You'll thank me later."

My whole body convulses as my orgasm washes over me. Maybe it's the long separation, or maybe it's his inhuman libido, but I have never come this hard in my entire life. I collapse onto the bed, burying my face in the duvet as I lose myself to the sensation. He probably comes to, but I'm so far gone, I don't even notice. Before I can fully recover, waves of exhaustion pulling me down, until I'm drowning in them.

* * *

I wake slowly, I don't know how long after, with Damien's arm wrapped around me. We're both tangled in his high thread count sheets, and I feel absolutely luxurious. His hand rests low on my back, steady and possessive. I breathe him in greedily. I've missed this so much.

I shift a little and feel him stir, his arm tightening instinctively.

"Good morning," I whisper.

He kisses the top of my head. "You slept hard," he answers back, stretching.

"I don't even remember falling asleep," I tell him honestly.

"I know," he chuckles. "I was worried I'd accidentally knocked you out, but then you started snoring."

I swat at his arm hard. "I do not snore!"

He laughs, louder this time. "Oh, you absolutely do!" he says, then does a very unflattering impression of what I definitely do not sound like. "But you needed the rest."

"I need my boyfriend to stop lying about me snoring," I grumble.

"Then text the guys," he smiles. "I'm sure they'll all back me up."

"I do not snore," I pout, crossing my arms like a petulant child.

Eventually, he convinces me to forgive him. A little with his lips and a lot with his hands, and we stay in bed for a little while longer. I'm not used to having such a lazy morning with him. Usually, he's up and ready to go before I've even opened my eyes, so I know that he's really moved his schedule around to take care of me. I feel like the luckiest woman alive.

Eventually, I untangle myself, slipping into his oversized robe and padding barefoot into the kitchen to make coffee. The sunlight is brighter now, painting the marble counters gold. It's beautiful here, high above the city, but I can't help but long for my tiny little flat in Paris.

I sip my coffee and lean against the counter, remembering that I left my phone in my bag. I walk over to the living room to grab it and see a dozen missed texts. I skim over them all, but one in particular catches my eye.

"Where are you? Are you alright?"

It's from Lucas, and it's his third text. My stomach lurches a little as I think about responding. What would I even say? We were barely friends. I don't want to tell him about what happened with Andre, because it still makes me feel so dirty. I don't want him thinking of me that way. So, I just leave the texts unread and decide I'll deal with them later.

I need to see McKenzie. We've both been so busy the last few weeks, I've barely had a chance to talk to her. She has no idea I'm home, and I can't wait to see her face, even though it means I'll have to explain why I'm home. But McKenzie is the one person I know will support me no matter what. I'm not worried about sharing everything with her.

When we get to my building, Damien carries my bag to the door, kisses me once, and lets me go. "I'll see you soon," he says.

I nod. "You'd better," I say, swatting at his ass as he walks away.

He turns back to wink at me, and I can't help but laugh.

When I push open the apartment door, McKenzie is in the kitchen in an oversized T-shirt and fuzzy socks, stirring something in a saucepan while singing along, badly, to some pop song.

I watch her for a second, trying to maintain my giggling.

"Do you always sing off-key, or is it just when you're alone?" I ask over the music.

She jumps, dropping the spoon into the pot with a splash. "Holy hell, Harper!"

I laugh and drop my bag. "Surprise."

She screams, runs across the kitchen, and tackles me into the world's tightest hug. "Oh, my God, you're home! You're actually home!"

"I'm home," I say, squeezing her just as tight.

She pulls back to look at me. "Wait. What happened? I thought you weren't coming back until December?"

"Change of plans," I shrug with a tired smile. "Want the short version or the full tea?"

She narrows her eyes. "Girl, I've got a full pot of cinnamon chai and nowhere to be. Sit your ass down."

We curl up on the couch, mugs in hand, blankets pulled up over our laps even though it's not that cold, and I start talking. I tell her everything.

Not just the surface-level version, but the real stuff. What it felt like to fall in love with Paris. The thrill of the art, the way the students made me feel like I had something to offer. The joy of wandering the streets with Rafe. The tension and excitement of being with Damien in a foreign city.

I tell her about Lucas. How sweet he was. How maybe I could've loved him in another life, or maybe I just needed him as a friend in this one. I tell her how we saw a play, walked arm in arm down cobbled streets, and how he kissed my hand instead of my mouth and made me blush like a schoolgirl.

And then I tell her the rest about Andre. About how quickly the air shifted in that room. How a perfectly normal conversation turned into something predatory and violating. How I told him to stop. How he didn't. How I pushed him and left and cried all the way home.

"Are you kidding me?" she says, clutching her mug like she might shatter it. "That asshole put his hands on you?"

I nod. "Please tell me Damien murdered him."

"He wanted to," I say, trying to smile. "But he at least got him fired."

"Good. How are you dealing with it all?"

I take a deep breath and exhale slowly. "Honestly, I think I'm okay.

I was more angry than anything. And tired. But I'm home now. That helps."

She pulls me into a hug. "I'm so sorry that happened."

"I know. But I'm glad to be back home with you."

She pulls back and wipes under her eyes. "Okay, okay," she sniffles. "Do your men know you're back?"

"Not yet," I say, reaching for my phone. "Let's fix that."

I shoot off a quick group text to Rafe, Scott, and Tomas. Then, after thinking about it for a few minutes, I message Melody.

Me: Hey. Just got home. Back in St. Paul. Missed you guys.

It takes less than thirty seconds for the first response.

Rafe: You're HOME??? I'm coming over.

Tomas: Where the hell have you been? I thought you were coming back in December. Are you okay?

Scott: I'll be there in ten. Do you want cinnamon rolls or flowers or both?

Melody: Omg welcome home. We have so much to talk about.

My phone keeps dinging. The screen floods with texts and emojis and exclamation points. McKenzie laughs so hard she nearly spills her tea. "You're the most popular girl in the entire state," she says.

I laugh too, because it feels good. Because it's the first time in days that something does.

17

ONE HECK OF A REUNION

Tomás

The second I see Harper, I forget how to breathe.

It's been over eight damn weeks since I've seen her or touched her or held her in my arms after a long night of making love to her perfect body. But when she sees me and smiles, it's like no time at all has passed.

Dios mío.

She's so fucking beautiful.

Her soft blue dress swishes around those perfect legs that I can't wait to wrap around my waist. Her hair spills down around her shoulders, just begging me to run my hands through it. I want to bury myself in the scent of her and fall apart while she screams my name.

"Hola, Profe," she says on an exhale.

"Helena," I murmur, stepping closer. I offer my arm like a gentleman, but my hand brushes her waist and lingers a second longer than necessary. "Estás preciosa."

She bats me away but then wraps her arms around my neck, pulling me into a tight hug. My own arms instinctively tighten around her waist, holding her to me as closely as I possibly can.

"Te extrañé mucho, mi amor," she whispers in my ear.

"I've missed you so fucking much," I breathe against her skin, no longer caring about being gentle.

We break apart briefly, but we don't stop touching all the way to the car. The moment she slips into the passenger seat, I have my hand on her knee passively, and she leans into me like she can't get enough. If I were less of a gentleman, I would walk her right back up to her apartment and show her exactly how much I've missed her, but I've been planning this romantic evening since the day she left.

Speaking of....

"So," I begin, unsure how much I should push her. "You're home early."

She takes a deep breath and tenses just a fraction before she grabs my hand and brings it to her lips. "I am," she confirms, but she says no more.

I wait patiently. I know my Harper well enough to know that she'll share whenever she's ready.

"Well I, for one, am so happy you are," I say, trying to lighten the atmosphere. "I've been losing my mind without you."

"Same," she smiles. "I was hoping our next romantic date would be in Paris, but I don't care where we are as long as we're together."

We're at an intersection now, and I kiss her briefly while the light is still red. It's chaste and sweet, and nothing like the way I want to kiss her. But we have so much time tonight for that. Right now, she needs some fun, and I hope to give her just that.

I pull into the small Argentinian restaurant I've been waiting for ages to bring her to. The food is divine, and I'm hoping she'll take this as an opportunity to practice her Spanish. Something about the way she rolls her Rs undoes me every time.

We're led to a small booth in the back of the restaurant, and she surprises me by sitting next to me, rather than across from me.

"I hope this is okay," she whispers in my ear. "I just didn't want to be so far away from you."

"Cariña," I whisper back, pulling her into another kiss. "You definitely don't have to apologize for that."

I wrap my arm around her and we sit snuggled into each other as the waitress comes to take our order. We barely break apart for the entire meal, except to feed each other bites of food.

"This churrasco is so tender," she nearly moans.

My dick stands at half-mast at the sound. Fuck, I need to touch her. "Try it with the chimichurri sauce," I tell her lowly. "You'll want to bathe in it."

Her eyes light up wickedly.

"Maybe we should take some home," she says mischievously. "And we can lick it off each other."

I can't help but laugh at her dirty mind. "Don't worry, amor," I chuckle. "I've got much sweeter sauces to lick off your body."

She takes a quick glance around the restaurant, then licks at the skin under my ear, biting lightly.

"Is it time for dessert yet?" she asks.

"You're going to make me do something that will get us banned from here permanently," I warn her teasingly.

Truthfully, I couldn't care less if we got banned from every restaurant in the tri-state area for indecent exposure. I need her like I need air to breathe.

"Then maybe we should get the check?" she suggests, and I immediately flag down the waitress.

It isn't until we're on the road back to my place that she starts to look more serious.

"I guess I should tell you about Paris now," she says thoughtfully. "Just so the air is completely clear between us."

I squeeze her knee gently, encouraging her to go on.

"My boss crossed a line," she says quietly. "Several, actually. I don't want to get into all of it, but he tried to come on to me. He tried to justify it because I was dating other men. He treated me like I was a common whore."

The words hit like a fist to my gut.

"Hijo de puta," I mutter, barely holding back the venom in my tone.

Harper's mouth lifts into a humorless smile. "I know," she answers, staring out the window. "Damien took care of it. He had the man fired, and he came to pick me up."

She looks back at me, and there's a hint of relief on her face. "But that's it. The whole sordid thing."

I sense there's more to it than that. There's a deep anger boiling under her skin that she doesn't seem willing to share with me. And how could she not be angry? Not only did that pendejo violate her, but he ruined her dream opportunity.

"I have some airline miles. We could fly to Paris right now and fuck him up."

She laughs at this genuinely and plants a sloppy kiss on my cheek. "There are a few things I'd much rather do right now than see that man again," she answers huskily.

To prove her point, she trails her hand along the tight seam of my pants. I can't drive home fast enough.

* * *

HARPER

The second Tomás's front door closes behind us, his mouth is on mine, and his hands are gathering fistfuls of my skirt and pulling the dress up my body.

"Helena," he breathes against my lips.

That one word is so desperate and wanting, I can't help but melt against him. I reach for the top of his shirt and start pulling to get the buttons loose.

"I missed you," I whisper, barely able to get the words out before he's kissing me again, his tongue pushing deep inside my mouth like he's trying to memorize the taste of me.

He manages to lift my dress over my head so that I'm standing in front of him in only my underwear. He groans when I finally push the fabric of his shirt aside and start kissing the exposed skin of his chest.

"Do you know how many nights I thought about this?" he

murmurs against my hair. "How many mornings I woke up reaching for you, only to remember you were across the ocean?"

I nod, too breathless to answer. Because I know. God, I know.

He lifts me like I weigh nothing and carries me to the bedroom. The moment my knees hit the mattress, I'm grabbing for the hooks of my bra to pull it off, and he's hooking his fingers through my panties, slowly dragging them down my legs.

"You're even more beautiful than my wildest fantasies," he says.

I reach for him, pulling him down with me. "And what did you fantasize about, exactly?" I challenge him. "Show me in perfect detail."

He nips at my bottom lip before using his fingers to spread my entrance and slipping a finger inside. I immediately arch against his touch.

"I dreamed about your hot, wet pussy," he groans as his finger starts moving fast inside of me. "How much I wanted to touch it and taste it and bury my cock deep inside of it."

"That all sounds really good," I manage to breathe, trying to match the rhythm of my hips to his punishing pace.

Just when I'm starting to climb toward the edge, he abruptly removes his finger. I whine at its absence, but when I meet his gaze and watch him suck my juices off his finger, I almost come right there.

"Fuck, Profe," I gasp, sitting up and grabbing at his hair. I kiss him soundly, rubbing my body against his. "I forgot how wet you make me."

"I didn't," he growls, as he quickly pulls down his pants and boxers. "I remember exactly how easy it is to slip inside of you."

I shiver at his words, but then he's pulling me against him, wrapping my legs around his waist as he slips into me. And, sure enough, it takes hardly any effort at all. I'm so ready to have him inside of me.

We both go still for a moment, forehead to forehead, our breath mingling, our hearts pounding in sync.

"I missed this so much," I whisper, because I need him to know. "Not just the sex, but how safe you make me feel."

His hips move, slow at first, like he wants to savor every second.

"Igualmente," he whispers back, as he starts slowly thrusting into me.

He feels the same.

Our rhythm builds slowly. Despite his need, he clearly wants to savor every second of this. He pulls out of me almost entirely before burying himself deep inside again. Each time, my head falls back, and he kisses the sensitive spot on my neck. He's building a hot, lasting fire inside of me.

He must be close, because he lays me down on the bed, cradling my face between his hands as he kisses me sloppily. My hips move to meet his, pulling him as deep inside of me as he can possibly go.

"I need you to touch me," I tell him, clutching at the sheets.

"Como así?" he asks, as he slowly circles my clit with one of his thumbs.

In no time at all, I'm seeing stars behind my eyes, and then he's collapsing on top of me, a string of curses falling from his lips.

"You never taught me those words, Profe," I joke.

He kisses me again, more tenderly.

* * *

THE NEXT MORNING, I WAKE UP TO THE SOUND OF CLINKING IN THE kitchen and the smell of something warm and buttery in the air. I keep my eyes closed a little longer, assessing the telltale aches in my body. I hope he's making a big breakfast, because I need it after last night.

"Buenos días, Profe," I murmur, my voice still scratchy from sleep when I finally emerge in the kitchen.

There's a huge plate of scrambled eggs and bacon, and he's heating up homemade tortillas. My stomach growls, and my mouth waters at the sight. I'm absolutely famished. I pick up a piece of bacon and have to physically stop myself from shoving the whole thing in my mouth.

"Hungry, amor?" Tomás laughs.

"Un poco," I shrug, before I sit at his counter and wait patiently for him to finish.

He finishes the tortillas and puts the plate next to the other, before he moves back to the kitchen to make me a cup of coffee. He knows exactly how I take it without asking, and that attention to detail is enough to make me melt.

Just as I'm about to ask him what he wants to do today, my phone rings. I pick it up and see Melody's picture flash across the screen. I try not to groan out loud as I answer it.

"Hey, Harp!" she says cheerily. "I was hoping you could take May for a couple of hours today."

I look over at Tomás, who's staring at me curiously.

"I kind of had plans today," I start slowly. "I don't know if I can take the baby."

Tomás's eyes go wide in excitement, and he nods.

"You want to babysit an infant today?" I ask him skeptically.

"It could be fun!" he says cheerfully. "Tell her we'll come pick her up in an hour."

"You guys are lifesavers!" Melody answers, clearly having heard him. "I'll see you then!"

We eat quickly and go pick up May at Melody's apartment. She won't let us inside, which I find curious. She just pushes May to us in her stroller and hands us her diaper bag.

"I'll come pick her up from your place in a few hours, okay?" Melody says again, too cheerfully.

"Sure," I say with a sinking feeling in my gut.

Tomás and I take May to the park, and then back to my apartment. We watch cartoons until she falls asleep, then we put on a movie and cuddle. By the time the movie is over, May is still sleeping, but I haven't heard a word from Melody.

I try to call her, but she doesn't answer. Tomás orders us dinner at some point, and I give May a bottle. Still no word from Melody. Once it gets dark outside, I really freak out. Tomás tells me he has to go, but he'll call to check on me in the morning. And still, there's no Melody.

When McKenzie gets home, we try to decide what to do.

We make May a little pallet on the floor with pool noodles on the side so she can't run into anything, and I try to ignore the panic growing in my chest that Melody isn't coming back to get her child.

18

ADVENTURES IN BABYSITTING

May's been fussy all night, and I still can't reach Melody. I try rocking the baby on my hip, trying to bounce and hum at the same time while brushing my teeth with my free hand. My toothbrush hits the back of my throat and I gag, which makes her scream louder.

"Jesus, May," I mumble around a mouthful of foam. "I'm trying."

I spit, rinse, and wipe my mouth on the nearest towel. My hair is a frizzy mess, and I haven't even touched my makeup yet. My shirt is damp from where May drooled all over it twenty minutes ago, and I smell like spit-up.

I glance at the clock. It's already 10:42 A.M., and I'm supposed to be at Scott's at noon. I've texted Melody five times and called her three. Nothing. Not even a read receipt. Just silence. And it's pissing me off.

"Okay," I say to May, shifting her to the other hip. "Let's try the bottle again. You have to work with me here."

She hiccups and stares up at me with wide eyes, like I'm the crazy one.

I try to bounce her on my knee and get her to take the bottle. She gurgles a little and starts sucking on it with disinterest. My phone dings, and I snatch it off the counter, hope rising in my chest. But it's not Melody.

It's McKenzie.

McKenzie: How's the baby chaos?

I roll my eyes and text back.

Me: She's still screaming and covered in spit. And Mel didn't give me a change of clothes. So it's going great.

Three dots appear.

McKenzie: Drop her at the studio. I can watch her for a bit.

Before I can respond, she sends another message.

I mean it. You deserve a break.

I chew on my lip. I'm torn. I'm supposed to see Scott today. We planned it a few days ago, and I need that time with him. But what do I do if Melody texts me finally? How will she feel about me leaving May with McKenzie?

After a short internal debate, I decide it doesn't matter. She's left me her child for over twenty-four hours and hardly enough resources to keep her alive. I'm going to have to break into her apartment soon if I don't hear back from Mel.

I call McKenzie. "Are you sure about this?"

"Yes," she says firmly. "You deserve some alone time with Scott."

"She's fussy," I warn.

"I've dated musicians," she laughs. "I can handle fussy."

"Where will you even put her?"

"I have a yoga mat and a huge scarf. I'll make her a nest."

I think about this for a minute before answering. "It can't be any worse than our pool noodle concoction."

"Exactly!" she chirps. "So, go see Scott, and let me see what I can do about Miss Fussy Pants."

McKenzie meets me outside the studio half an hour later. She's got her giant bag slung over her shoulder, sunglasses on, and a scarf already tied into a makeshift baby sling.

"Hand her over," she commands, holding her arms out to a wiggly May.

She immediately quiets down and snuggles into McKenzie's shoulder with a happy sigh.

"Traitor," I mutter.

McKenzie laughs at me. "There's no replacement for good taste," she shrugs. "Now get out of here or you'll be late!"

"Text me if anything happens," I tell her. "And if Melody shows up—"

"I'll tell her to get her shit together," she cuts me off. "Who the hell would dump such a sweet little girl on her unsuspecting friend?"

Her last sentence is in baby talk, and completely focused on May, who lets out a little giggle. They're clearly happy together, so I feel less guilty about leaving them for my date with Scott. By 11:55, I'm standing outside his door, my hair still slightly damp and a suspicious stain on my shirt that I can't worry about. Because approximately half a second later, he opens the door and pulls me inside.

Half a second after that, I'm pinned against the door with his mouth on mine, his tongue hungrily searching my mouth. He only pulls away when my stomach growls so loudly it can't be ignored. And then Milo is bounding toward us, all puppy energy and no grace, and the three of us end up in a heap on the floor.

I laugh happily as I pull my sweet boy against my chest and place kisses all over his face. Milo, that is. Scott watches us with adoration in his eyes.

"How've you been?" he asks as he pulls Milo away and tries to calm him down.

"Right this second, I'm doing better than I have in ages," I answer honestly, not wanting to bring down our day with all the recent drama in my life.

"Agreed!" he answers automatically. "But I don't think you left Paris just to see me."

"Of course not," I quip. "I left Paris because I missed Milo so much."

Upon hearing his name, Milo jumps back into my lap and starts licking my face.

"Okay, Milo," Scott groans. "Let your mama get up and get some lunch."

Milo turns sharply and stares at Scott with his head cocked. Clearly, "lunch" is one of his trigger words.

Scott and I get up and go to the kitchen, where he has a spread of cold cuts, fresh fruit, and an assortment of delicious-looking cheeses waiting for us. My stomach growls again, and I suddenly realize that I never had breakfast this morning. I was too busy trying to wrangle May to even think about it.

"So," Scott starts slowly. "You don't have to tell me why you really came home. But I do want to know what's really going on with you. Don't sugarcoat anything for me, baby."

I melt at his words. I turn to find him standing nearer to me than I realized, and I immediately wrap my arms around his neck. Unable to stop myself, I lean up and kiss him again, more tenderly this time.

"I'm not even sure where to start," I answer honestly.

We both stack up our plates with sandwiches and fruit and sit down at his kitchen table. Milo lays down very sweetly underneath, and I'm beyond impressed by how well-trained he already is.

I take small bites and try to explain everything to Scott. Rehashing Paris gets a little easier every time I talk about it, and I think I'll actually be able to move on from it soon. Who knows? Maybe I'll try to go back one day, now that Andre is out of the picture.

The May issue is much more tender. I'm so frustrated with Melody for abandoning her daughter. She still hasn't gotten in touch with me, and all my messages are going unread.

"Who the hell would abandon their baby?" he asks, a tinge of anger in his voice.

"Tell me about it," I groan. "And she didn't just abandon her. She gave me nothing. I have a diaper bag with maybe three diapers left. That won't get us through the night."

As I say it, panic grips me as I consider that Melody might actually leave May with me for another night. What the hell is going on with her?

"Considering everything you're going through, you still look fine as shit," he smirks at me over his glass of lemonade. "I think that outfit would look great on my bedroom floor."

"Be serious, Scott," I fake chastise.

He looks at me with surprise and a little guilt before I smile at him.

"When do we ever make it to your bedroom?"

He laughs. "Good point."

He pulls me onto his lap, with my legs straddling him. Now that I'm fed, I can focus more on what's really important, and that's having this gorgeous man underneath me. I rake my hands through his hair as I grind against him. It takes him no time at all to get hard underneath me, and I'm already wet in anticipation of his big dick inside of me. No one stretches me quite like he does.

I moan against his lips as he begins as he gently cups my breasts. It's not enough, and he must agree. He grabs my hips and moves me off of him so I'm sitting on the edge of the table. Then he's kissing me again, but our hands move in a flurry as we each strip off our clothing.

Just like I anticipated.

He pulls me as close to the edge of the table as he can to line us up, and then he's inching in slowly. I gasp as my body tries to get used to him again. It's been so long, my body has to learn how to stretch around him again, but I relish in the feeling. He's so damn patient with me.

Once he's fully sheathed, he starts moving, and soon the table is scraping against the floor as it moves with us. Milo starts barking, and we can only laugh, but we don't stop. I don't think either of us could if we wanted to.

It's equally quick and shattering. His dick is so big, it hits all the right spots, pulling pleasure out of me effortlessly. He falls apart first, but he's conscious enough to finish me with his fingers. I love that he knows me so well. I love that I don't have to tell him—he just knows exactly how to get me off.

We finish in a matter of minutes, and thank goodness, because Milo is growling and whining at us like he's about to lose his mind.

We quickly re-dress and give him the attention he's desperately asking for, assuring him that everything is okay."

It's more than okay, actually. It's perfect.

But then my phone buzzes, and I'm reminded that this is just a piece of my life. Somewhere a few miles away, my best friend is babysitting my other friend's daughter, and said friend is MIA.

I frown as I look at the phone.

"Is everything okay?" Scott asks as he clears the plates off the table.

"McKenzie just sent me a picture of her and May," I say. "She's having the time of her life."

"That's a good thing, right?" he asks casually.

"It would be better if I knew that Melody was coming back for May in a few hours," I sigh. "I should probably get back and relieve McKenzie of babysitting duty."

"You're a really good friend, Harper," he tells me earnestly.

He pulls me into another kiss, though it's more chaste. He knows I'm leaving, and he can't convince me to stay with sex. I mean, he could, if he really wanted to. But the gnawing guilt in the back of my head wouldn't go away.

"I'll see you soon, okay?" I promise him.

"The sooner, the better," he says with a smile before kissing me one last time.

When I get to the studio, McKenzie and May are snuggling together on top of a giant canvas. It's a strange picture seeing the two of them lying there. May is swaddled in her baby blanket, sound asleep. I swear, McKenzie may actually be the baby whisperer.

"Okay," McKenzie says without sitting up. "I've decided I want one."

"A baby?"

"May specifically."

I laugh quietly, trying not to wake her. "You might get your wish," I answer wryly.

"Still no word from Mel?" she asks, turning carefully to look up at me.

"Nothing," I groan. "What are we going to do?"

"Well, she definitely needs more formula," McKenzie confirms, adding to my growing concerns. "And I think I used her last diaper."

"Shit," I say under my breath. "What are we going to do?"

"I'd suggest we call the police, but I don't want this sweet little thing to end up in the system."

"Me neither," I agree. "I have Mel's spare key. Maybe she's at home, and I can just leave May there. But even if she's not, I can grab a few things."

May stirs, and we both look down at her. I carefully scoop her up and put her in her carrier so I can take her back home, even if it's just for a few minutes.

19

———

PUT ME IN, COACH

Rᴀꜰᴇ

Cold air hits me as soon as I step outside for practice. Fall is definitely turning into Winter, and soon our games are going to be brutal. It doesn't bother me today, though. Maybe it's because the Vikings are sitting on our best record in years, and the Super Bowl's within our reach. Or maybe it's because Harper's back in town.

Once practice is over, I get in my truck, crank the heat, and pull up her contact. The only thing that could make this weekend better would be seeing my girl. But when she answers on the third ring, she sounds exhausted. I'm shocked to hear a baby crying in the background.

"Is there something you forgot to tell me?" I joke.

"Don't even start," she snaps grumpily. "Melody's basically abandoned her daughter here. I'm on day three with no idea when or if she's even coming back."

"What the fuck?" I curse. "Are you okay?"

"I don't know," she answers honestly, and I hear the stress in her voice. "May's been fussy all morning. I think she hates me. I'm at my wit's end, I really don't know what to do."

I grip the wheel and exhale, so angry at Mel for dumping her daughter on Harper. Melody isn't my favorite person anyway after she ruined our relationship the first time by lying and saying I slept with her. I thought a few years might help her mature, but it seems like she's back to abusing Harper's kindness.

"I'm coming over," I tell her firmly. "Give me twenty, and then you're getting a break."

"What? No, Rafe, you don't have to—"

"I want to," I cut her off. "And you can't stop me."

She doesn't respond right away, but when she finally does with a small, "Okay," I swear I hear her sniffling.

I hate Mel for this. Harper's done nothing but support her, despite what a toxic bitch she can be. This is classic her. I was worried when Harper's parents insisted that she help Melody when she was pregnant, and now all my concerns are justified. Three days of no contact is nuts. Of course, this is Mel we're talking about. She's certifiably insane.

When I get to Harper's place, she looks even more exhausted than she sounded. Her hair is piled in a messy bun on top of her head, and she has dark circles under her eyes. She's wearing one of my old T-shirts, and it's covered in something.

My anger at Mel surges all over again. Harper shouldn't be dealing with all this stress, especially so soon after coming home from Paris.

I'm so focused on Harper, I barely notice the angry, red-faced baby squirming in her arms. But then the little girl opens her mouth and starts screaming, demanding notice.

"Well, that's one way to say hello," I tell May in mock offense.

Harper moves aside to let me in without a word, all the while bouncing May on her hip to try to calm her. "Don't take it personally," she says, almost hysterically. "Screaming is her primary form of communication."

"Put me in, coach," I say, holding out my hands for May.

Harper eyes me skeptically. "Rafe, you really don't have to," she protests. "Nothing works on this kid. She's had a fresh bottle, I just changed her, and I keep trying to make her laugh. Nothing works."

"Harper, I can handle a screaming baby for a few minutes," I argue. "You look like you could use those minutes for yourself. I've got this."

"Are you sure?" she asks, hesitant.

"I'm positive," I confirm, taking May from her arms.

I tuck the baby against my chest, holding her like a touchdown football. She starts to hiccup, and I remember something I saw one of my teammates do once with his kid. I flip May over so she's resting her little tummy on my forearm, and I start gently patting her back. Within a few seconds, she lets out a long, loud burp, and she immediately calms down.

Harper watches us in amazement. "How the hell did you do that?"

I can't help but grin. I've never considered myself good with kids, but I always relish the chance to impress my girl. "There are lots of little Vikings," I laugh. "I guess I've picked up a few tips."

Harper collapses on the couch like her legs have given out. She stares at me with glassy eyes, and I can see that she's seconds away from weeping. I've seen that look on her a few times in my life, and I don't like it at all.

"Go take a bubble bath," I suggest. "A long one, with lots of bubbles. And, if you need a nap, take one. May and I will be just fine."

She looks like she's about to argue, but when May fusses again, she thinks better of it. She just nods and turns toward her room.

"Now, Miss May," I say, holding her up to my face so we can see each other eye to eye. "We're going to figure out what makes you happy."

She stares at me for two seconds before she screams again.

By the time Harper emerges an hour and a half later, I've managed to get May to sleep against my chest, and I have on a game on the TV.

"Did you drug her?" Harper asks suspiciously.

She comes to sit next to us, her hair still damp, but she looks completely refreshed. I wrap my arm around her and pull her into the cuddlefest.

"Nah, she's just like you," I murmur. "I put on a soccer game and she knocked right the fuck out."

Harper lets out a genuine laugh, and my heart soars knowing

that I could provide her some amount of relief. She's definitely more relaxed than when I first arrived. We get almost a full hour of quiet while May sleeps, and we dare not do anything to wake her up.

At some point, Harper starts to doze against my chest as well, and I can't help but chuckle. Soccer works every time.

When McKenzie bursts through the door in the early evening, she stops short, her eyes lighting up at the sight of me sprawled on the couch with two sleeping girls on my chest.

"Well, isn't this wholesome as hell," she says, kicking off her boots.

"If you wake her up, I'll murder you," Harper mutters, her voice muffled in my shirt.

McKenzie tilts her head. "You two need a break," she says, carefully scooping May off my chest without waking her. "I'll take the night shift."

"McKen—" Harper begins.

"Go," she insists, cutting her off and waving us toward the door. "I've been dying for some baby time all day!"

* * *

HARPER

I should feel guilty about how fast I change once McKenzie practically pushes us out the door, but I don't. For the first time in days, the weight on my shoulders feels lighter. I slip into a deep green wrap dress and boots, barely bothering with makeup. When I step back into the living room, Rafe's waiting by the door, looking effortlessly attractive.

He straightens when he sees me, his eyes sparking like fire. He whistles lowly. "Damn, Ward," he breathes. "You look hot as fuck."

Heat rises to my cheeks. "I figured I'd try to look human again."

He closes the space between us, his thumb grazing my jaw, his voice rough. "You look like hot," he says, just loud enough for me to hear.

"Get a room, you two," McKenzie shouts in disgust. "Preferably one that isn't in this apartment."

She doesn't have to tell us twice.

He takes me to a slightly casual Chinese restaurant a few blocks away.

"I wanted to do something a little more romantic, but you look like you just need something quick and filling."

"You know me so well," I smile. "This is perfect!"

Rafe orders wine for me, and a beer for himself. We sip slowly, letting the alcohol unwind us after a full afternoon of watching a teething May.

"Better?" he asks, watching me over the rim of his glass.

"So much better." And I mean it.

He tells me all about his season, and I feel guilty for only slightly paying attention to it. It was easier to follow his season when he was in San Francisco. In fairness, though, his first few games happened while I was in a different time zone.

I try desperately to talk about anything besides May and Melody. It's weighing heavily on me right now. I did manage to get into her apartment and grab some things to make May more comfortable at my place. The apartment was a bit of a disaster, and Melody was nowhere to be found. I ended up having a meltdown in the middle of the living room, imagining what it would be like if Melody doesn't come back.

"Talk to me, Ward," Rafe commands, pulling me out of my thoughts.

"It's nothing," I lie.

"You're worried about Melody not coming home," he reads my mind. "Because you know she has it in her to fully abandon her child."

"That's not fair," I try to argue, but it's half-hearted at best. We both remember how thoroughly she ruined our relationship so many years ago.

"What's not fair is asking you to babysit and then disappearing for three days. She could be arrested for that shit."

"They'd have to find her first," I laugh humorlessly.

His jaw tenses, but instead of arguing, he lifts my hand to his lips and presses a kiss to the back of it. "You've always had a heart too big for your own good."

"I thought you liked that about me."

"I do," he says softly, his smile melting me from the inside out. "It's just hard watching it wear you down."

We finish our meal in relative silence after that, both consumed with our own thoughts. But it's still comfortable. That's the thing about being with someone you've known most of your life. We don't feel the need to fill every second with words.

But, of course, it makes me forget who Rafe is to the rest of the world. And I'm sharply reminded when we step out of the restaurant to a string of bright flashes.

Paparazzi.

Rafe curses under his breath and shifts instantly, his broad shoulders blocking me from their lenses.

"I shouldn't have taken you out this close to the stadium district," he mutters. "I wasn't even thinking."

My pulse pounds, the old sense of panic clawing at the back of my throat. But I force myself to breathe. I slide my hand onto his arm. "It's okay."

"Is it?" His voice is tight, protective.

I nod, even though my heart's still racing. "Nothing could ruin my night with you," I tell him.

He leans in and kisses me on the sidewalk while flipping off the paparazzi. We slip back into the night, the flashes chasing us until the car doors shut.

By the time we're back at his apartment, all I want is to express my thanks for how he stepped in today. How he always steps in.

"I missed you," I breathe, the words lost against his mouth as I kiss him.

His groan vibrates through me, his hands sliding under my dress with a hunger that makes my knees go weak. He lifts me like I weigh nothing and carries me over to the couch. Neither one of us have enough patience to go to the bedroom.

He yanks the dress off in one smooth motion, his eyes burning over me like he's been starving. His mouth follows, kissing a pattern down my throat, over my chest, down my stomach until he's dragging off my underwear and kissing my center.

I gasp when his fingers slip between my thighs, teasing until I'm clutching the fabric of the couch, begging for more.

"Take off your pants," I whisper with a gasp, trying to hold on to my sanity.

He somehow manages to take off his pants with one hand, never stopping his ministrations on my soaked pussy.

"I'm glad we didn't order dessert," he groans. "You're much sweeter."

I moan and lift my hips to get more friction. But then I remember that I'm the one who's supposed to be making him feel good after everything he's done for me.

"Stop," I order reluctantly.

He looks up with no small amount of surprise and concern, but I push him away. Then I'm standing, grabbing his hand and guiding him down on the couch so I can show him exactly how grateful I am for everything he's done.

"Harper," he moans, almost in protest.

"Shh," I command. "I want to show you exactly how much you mean to me."

I straddle him, taking him in one quick motion. His head falls back against the couch as I ride him. His hands grab my hips, but otherwise, he's completely lost in his pleasure. It's unbelievably sexy watching him try to hold on to his last ounce of control.

"Come inside me, baby," I order again. "I want to watch you fall apart."

His body shudders as his orgasm overtakes him, and I feel him let go inside of me. I keep riding him until I find my release—before I collapse on top of him.

2 0

A LITTLE HELP

Harper

Rafe holds me gently and runs his fingers lazily down my spine. I could stay here all night, I really could, but I'm not going to abandon May the same way her mother did. The last thing she needs is more disruption to her life.

"Rafe," I whisper.

His hand stills. "Hmm?"

"I have to go."

He tightens underneath me. "Already?"

I nod against his skin and force myself upright. "I don't want to leave McKenzie alone too long," I explain. "She's great with May, but this isn't her responsibility. It's mine."

"It actually isn't yours," he argues. "It's Melody's."

He shifts so I am looking at him. He gives me a teasing grin, but the concern in his eyes is real. "I could stay at your place," he suggests. "Make you breakfast in bed tomorrow. Take the morning shift with May."

"You have an early practice tomorrow," I remind him. "It's so sweet of you to offer, but you shouldn't put your life on hold too."

"I don't mind," he says earnestly. "You know I would do anything for you."

"I do," I agree, nodding. "But would you do anything for Melody? Because, ultimately, she's who you're helping."

His nose crinkles up like he's smelling something bad. "That's a good point," he concedes. "May is cute, but she's literally the spawn of Satan."

"Rafe," I warn him. "We don't choose who our parents are. And Melody and I have made up."

"That doesn't mean I have to forgive her," he grumbles. "And it doesn't mean she isn't Satan."

I can't help but laugh, and I kiss him gently as I move to get up. "I'll call you when this is all figured out, okay?" I promise him.

"Fine," he groans. "Leave me high and dry."

I roll my eyes. "You and I both know you just had a mind-blowing orgasm. Don't be such a whiner."

He fake pouts, but helps me gather my clothes. When we're both fully dressed, he grabs my hand and walks me to his car. We don't talk much on the way. My mind is preoccupied, wondering what horrible thing might have happened to Melody. There's no way she just needed a little break from motherhood, not for three days with no calls and texts. Something could be seriously wrong.

Outside my apartment, Rafe gives me one last long, lingering kiss, and grumbles again about how selfish Melody is being. I don't try to argue, mostly because I'm really hoping it's just selfishness and not something much worse.

"Welcome home, Auntie Harper," McKenzie says in a high-pitched, creepy voice when I walk in the door.

"Auntie Harper?" I ask curiously.

"We're workshopping," she shrugs, pointing to where May is fast asleep in her pack and play crib.

"Thank you," I say, dropping my bag and kissing the top of May's head. "Again."

"It is fine," she says happily. "She only woke up for a little while after you left. She must have tuckered herself out from all that screaming she did all last night."

"Let's hope she stays asleep," I say with a sigh.

She kicks in her sleep, and my stomach clenches, worried she's going to wake up, but she just gurgles and turns her head before exhaling and getting back to her little baby dreams.

"I think it's time to talk about the long term," McKenzie starts carefully. "It's fun pretending we're co-parenting a baby, but we have to find Melody. Neither of us is equipped to take care of May permanently."

"I've been thinking the same," I agree. "I'm going to call Damien tomorrow and see if he has some resources we can use. I don't want to go to the police."

"This is scaring me," she says. "Are you sure we shouldn't file a missing person report?"

I shake my head. "Not yet," I sigh heavily. "I don't think she's missing. I think she just doesn't want to be found. You didn't see her before I left for Paris. She was really struggling."

"But what if she's hurt?" she argues. "I mean, it's possible that something awful happened, and she didn't just abandon May with you."

"Maybe." I shrug. "But if we file a missing person report and it turns out she's just taken herself on a mini holiday without notice, they might take May away from her."

McKenzie stares at me pointedly for a second, and I hear what she isn't saying. Maybe May *should* be removed from Melody's care if this is how she's going to behave. But I just shake my head again.

"She needs help," I argue, though I might just be arguing with myself. "Damien can help us find her, and then we can help get her some real care."

In the meantime, I carefully pick May up as McKenzie picks up the pack and play and tries to silently drag it into my room. Miraculously, we manage to settle her back in without waking her, and I let out a sigh of relief.

Yet even as tired as I am, it takes me a long time to settle down, even after a shower and a nice cup of sleepy tea. I lie in the dark with my phone in my hand and stare at my unread texts to Melody. Her last text to me was asking me to come watch May.

I type out a message.

Where are you? Please tell me you are okay.

I delete it. I type it again. I delete it again.

I call, but it goes straight to voicemail. I wipe away the tears that I didn't realize were starting to fall.

May stirs at six the next morning. I change her diaper and carry her into the kitchen to make a bottle for her and a cup of coffee for myself. My body aches from carrying her around for the last three days, and I do have a certain appreciation for what Mel must be going through. It's hard doing this alone, and I've actually had a lot of support.

I put May in her pack and play, along with some soft toys so she can practice her grabbing skills, and get to the task at hand. By 10:00 A.M., I've called three hospitals, two police departments, and the only women's shelter I can think of. No one has seen anyone matching her description. It's both a relief and a disappointment. At least she's not hurt or in a jail cell. But then, where the hell is she?

I try her cell again and nearly scream when it goes to voicemail. "Melody, it is Harper. I'm not mad at you. I just need you to let me know you're safe."

I look down at May. She gazes back up at me with a toothless smile and starts laughing. That's it. I can't let this go on for another hour. May needs her mother. I scroll to Damien's contact and press call. He answers on the first ring.

"Hello, my little red bird," he answers affectionately.

"I need your help," I say by way of greeting, feeling a little desperate.

"You have it," he responds immediately.

"Remember my friend Melody?" I ask, as if he could forget. It's not every day you drive a pregnant woman to the hospital in your town car. At least, I assume it's not. "She asked me to watch her baby three days ago, and then she just vanished. She's not responding to any calls or texts, and I'm worried something bad might have happened."

"Have you filed a police report?" he asks.

"I'm worried that they'll take May away from her," I say in a small voice.

"It's sweet of you to worry like that," he answers kindly. "But if something is wrong, we need their help to find her. And if it comes to it, I can loan her the use of my lawyer. And, just in case, I'll put my PI on it to see if he can find her before the police do."

"Thank you, Damien," I say in a rush of air. "This whole situation has been such a nightmare."

"I bet," he mutters. "Listen, you don't need to be dealing with this on your own. I'm sending you over a nanny to help with her so you can get back to your life."

"You don't have to do that," I protest. "We're doing okay."

"Harper," he says forcefully. "It's better not to argue with me on this. She'll be there in an hour. Besides, who else will take care of the baby when I take you to the orchestra tomorrow?"

I can't help but smile at his way of insisting, rather than asking, me to go on a date with him. Of course I agree. And for the first time since I last saw Melody, I finally have some hope.

As promised, Gabriela, the nanny, shows up at my door one hour later. Under one arm, she carries a large box that I just know is an expensive dress.

"Mr. Blackwood said I could kill two birds with one stone," she tells me, shrugging. "He said you'd know what that means."

"Thank you." I chuckle, taking the heavy box from her and showing her around the small apartment.

"I don't know if Mr. Blackwood explained the situation," I begin, not used to using his formal name. "My friend left her baby with me. I have no idea if I'm even taking care of her right."

"You've kept her alive for three days," Gabriela answers kindly. "You've given her a comfortable home and plenty of affection. You're doing better than you think."

"Thank you," I say, a little teary-eyed.

"Now," she says, picking up May. "Why don't you let the two of us get acquainted, and you can go take care of whatever you need to do."

I feel weird leaving a stranger in my house with May, so I spend most of the day tidying up the disaster my apartment has become and making more phone calls. Damien has texted me the police case number, and his PI has texted me to let me know he'll be updating me as soon as he knows something. There's nothing left to do but relax and wait.

The next evening, Gabriela assures me that she can handle May while I go to the orchestra. I've been able to observe her with May for a day and a half, and she's definitely legit. May is the happiest I've ever seen her, and she's hardly been fussy at all.

Damien picks me up outside my apartment, dressed impeccably in black tie. The dress he sent over fits like a glove, and he watches me with dark eyes as I approach.

"I believe I've outdone myself," he says happily, pulling me in for a quick kiss.

In the car, we can barely keep our hands to ourselves, though I make him promise not to ruin my makeup. I don't want to get to the orchestra looking like a train wreck. All too soon, we're pulling up to the venue, and I have to practically push Damien away so we can go inside.

But I have to admit, I love the way he's so attentive.

The performance is gorgeous. Damien has a private box that overlooks the stage, and we listen to the stunning pieces as he holds my hand. It's like listening to a painting. Each instrument overlaps and interweaves with the others, creating this cacophony that shouldn't work together but does. By the end of the performance, I feel breathless, and I shoot out of my seat for a standing ovation.

Damien chuckles beside me, a little slower getting out of his seat and a little less enthusiastic. But he can't tamper my excitement. This is far too fun for me.

I stand by as he shakes the hands of some important people in his box, though his hand never leaves my waist. I'm his arm candy, and I don't mind it one bit. When I'm with Damien, I feel important just by proximity.

"These people are all so insufferable," he whispers in my ear when we finally have a chance to make a break for it.

I can't help but giggle, especially because Damien initiated several of the conversations. "You think everyone is insufferable," I tease.

"Everyone except you." He smiles, giving me a quick peck on the cheek.

He leads me out toward the car, where there's a gaggle of paparazzi waiting to photograph him. He puts his hands up to shield us, but I already have the sinking feeling in my stomach that I'll be getting a nasty phone call sometime this week from my mom.

It's all worth it, though.

"Even they can't keep their eyes off of you," Damien murmurs in my ear when we get in the car.

"They're here because of you," I remind him. "I'm just the mystery girl everyone is gossiping about."

"One day, the whole world will know who you are," he says against the skin of my neck, giving me goosebumps. "And people will wonder who the decrepit old man next to her is."

I throw my head back and laugh, trying to imagine a world where Damien isn't the most handsome man in the room.

It's impossible.

I sigh as we turn onto my street, regretful that I can't spend more time with him, but I want to let Gabriela go home.

"I'm making the search for Melody my top priority," he says under his breath when the car stops. "That way, I can keep you all night."

2 1

EMOTIONAL RELEASE

Harper

Sure enough, my picture is all over the tabloids the following morning. I sigh as I chew my cereal and scroll through my phone while May takes her morning nap. If nothing else, at least it's a good picture of me. The dress Damien bought really accentuates my curves, and the color is gorgeous against my skin. I look like someone much more glamorous than I actually am.

I scroll through a few more articles and see pictures of Rafe and me at the restaurant the other night. I had no clue they were taking pictures of us in the restaurant. We look cozy, though, and happy together. Rafe is laughing at something I've said, while I take a sip of my drink. We're the picture of domesticity.

"Who is this Mystery Woman?" echoes most of the headlines.

"Is Bullet Maloney a Cuckold?" asks one.

"Apparently Damien Blackwood Does Know How to Share," reads another.

I roll my eyes, but the pictures are everywhere. Even on social media, I'm confronted with my face and a barrage of nasty comments underneath. It takes me all of five minutes to decide that I won't read them. The ones I do see are nasty enough to ruin my week.

Not as much as my parents can, though. The second my phone vibrates. and I see Mom's face flash on my screen, I know I'm in for it.

"I'm not talking about this," I say instead of hello.

"We are going to talk about it," I hear my dad huffing, though his voice is far away. Mom probably has the phone on speaker. "What the hell are you doing with your life, Harper? This isn't who we raised you to be."

I roll my eyes again and settle in for the reprimand.

"Sweetie," my mom cuts in, trying to sound more compassionate and less aggressive. "You have to understand how this makes us look. This isn't just your life you're playing with. It's ours too."

"How exactly am I playing with your life?" I ask, a little harshly.

"You know how," she says blandly. "It was one thing when there were just two pictures. We could easily just explain it away and say that you're just friends with this Damien person. But now there are more photos, and they're both from this week!"

"So what?" I ask. "The only people who need to worry about who I'm seen with are me and them." I purposely keep my language vague so I don't accidentally slip that there are two other men in the equation.

"How can you be so selfish?" Dad nearly screams. His face is probably purple by now. "Do you realize how bad this makes us look? Our daughter is out there whoring herself out to two very powerful men and–"

"First of all–" I cut him off, my heart beating so loud I can hear it pounding in my ears. "I am not 'whoring myself out.' Let's be very clear about that. I am in consensual relationships with men who care about me very much, and I care very much about them."

"Harper," Mom starts, but I don't let her interrupt.

"Second of all, my love life isn't your business unless I make it your business. And, trust me, I am never going to make it your business. You've made it pretty clear that you don't trust me to know myself, and that's fine. But don't expect me to share anything about my relationships with you at all."

"Young lady, this is not up for discussion," Dad cuts in.

"You're right." I can't help but laugh. "It's not up for discussion. And, by the way, I have enough going on in my life without you trying to lecture me. Did you know that Melody just abandoned May here?"

My mother gasps in shock and I know that she, at least, will now be too mentally preoccupied to worry about my dating habits.

"And now that I'm home from Paris, I need to get back to painting," I continue. "But I can't find the time to paint because I'm too busy taking care of May."

"Harper, that's awful," my mother says sympathetically, and I know she's giving my dad one of those looks that makes him immediately shut up.

"It is awful!" I confirm. "And what's worse is I have no idea where Melody is. I haven't been able to get her to answer her phone for days. So excuse me if I'm trying to find a little bit of happiness right now, and excuse me if I don't give a damn what the two of you think about it!"

I hang up before I can overthink what I'm doing and put my phone on Do Not Disturb. I know they'll try to call me back, but I don't want to deal with the drama anymore. I'm over it. I put my bowl in the sink, and right then, I hear Gabriela knocking. Perfect timing.

I let her take over while I go to the studio and try to get some work done. Leaving Paris really did leave a void in my life and in my work, and I've barely been able to process any of it. McKenzy is already in the studio, her headphones in while she works on staining a table. I set myself up on my side of the room and stare at a blank canvas for a while.

I'm still so angry with my parents. They have a lot of nerve trying to guilt me for enjoying my life. All my life, they tried to break me, to form me into the perfect, obedient daughter who never stepped out of line and never embarrassed them. I spent so much time carrying so much shame because I was afraid to do anything outside of their rules.

I dip my paintbrush in a dark red and start pulling it across the canvas, leaving streaks of paint that feel dark and different from anything I've done before. Before I know it, I'm staring at a self-portrait in dark shades of red, gray, black, and orange. It looks like it's bleeding. It feels alive with rage and anger, but there's so much more underneath the surface.

I add in some lighter accents before stepping away and deciding it's perfect. It's exactly how I'm feeling, like a reborn version of myself who's no longer afraid to acknowledge and show how much damage my upbringing did to me.

I set aside the canvas to dry and realize that it only took a couple hours. The sun is still high in the sky, and McKenzy is still working on her table. She has barely even looked up at me, lost in her own piece. And the rage inside of me is still there.

I grab another canvas and start sketching out the Paris skyline. It's harsh and a little jagged, nothing like the gorgeous interpretations I've seen from every other artist. It's nothing like the Paris I spent two months in. The feel is colder and darker, and there's a level of fear there. It's how Andre made me feel when he tried to come on to me. He ruined Paris for me, and I find a way to express that on the canvas.

Again, it just pours out of me, and again I'm shocked to realize how little time it took. Sometimes it takes me days to finish one painting, and I've just channeled all of these negative feelings into two slightly unhinged versions of my life. They're different than anything I've painted before, but they're real and raw and they make me feel everything I've been trying to suppress.

I grab another canvas and start painting again, not paying much attention to the tears coming down my face. By the time I finish the last one, the sky is just getting darker, and McKenzy is gone. She must have taken one look at my face and known to leave me be. I stretch my sore muscles and take a look at the final piece.

It's a woman walking away from a child. Her face is half-turned back, and there's so much pain and despair on it. The child is sleeping, unaware that it's just been abandoned, making the visual story so much more interesting. I finally wipe away the tears that have been gathering, and I immediately think of Melody.

She must have been so much pain to even consider leaving May. That's not something a healthy, functioning person would do. Wherever she is, she's hurting, and May is too young to have any idea that her world is upside down.

When I get back to the apartment, I pick May up and squeeze her tight. She whines and squirms, but I don't care. I want her to understand that she's loved. Not just by me, but by Melody too, wherever she might be.

I work on the series more over the next few days, until I feel completely empty inside. Every painting represents a significant emotion I've been feeling. There's another distorted self-portrait, this one representing how all this media coverage makes me hardly recognize myself anymore. There's another painting of a woman trying to run away from a dark, shadowy monster as she runs toward a freeing light.

There are more paintings of various places in Paris, and a few of Barcelona. Some are happy and hopeful, while others are warped and almost scary. I take in the series as a whole and see so much of my life in the stories here. I call Damien and ask if he'll come take a look.

"Wow," is all he says, and I'm proud that I've left him speechless.

"Good wow, or bad wow?" I can't help but ask.

"Wow," he says, turning to me with a smile on his face. "Incredible."

I blush a little and let him pull me in for a quick kiss, but the affection is fast because he's Damien. He can't just appreciate the art without finding someone to display the art. He calls some friend who owns a gallery in Seattle and asks if he can send over some snapshots.

"He wants to do an exhibition," he tells me a few minutes later. "Are you okay with that?"

I look back at the paintings and know that they deserve to be out in the world. They're finished, and I want to send them on with the peace of knowing that I'm going to be okay. I've battled my demons on the canvas and clearly won.

* * *

TWO WEEKS LATER, I DROP MAY OFF WITH MY PARENTS. THEY STILL aren't thrilled with me, but they won't deny May anything. She might as well be their granddaughter for how much they dote on her.

Damien whisks me away to Seattle for the opening, and it's so surreal. I've seen my paintings in a gallery before, of course, but not one where I didn't have to pay ridiculously for the space. Damien's friend liked my paintings so much, he made the offer. He's taking care of the whole thing, and he's invited me to the opening as the guest of honor.

"The opening is sold out," Damien tells me on the plane. It's overwhelming and exciting to hear. "There's a lot of buzz about your paintings, little red bird."

The opening itself is such a whirlwind of activity. Damien wasn't kidding. The place is packed. I fade into the crowd, listening to all the positive feedback about the pieces, relishing in the anonymity for a while. Eventually, I'm introduced as the artist, and so many strangers come up to congratulate me and tell them how seen my paintings make them feel.

"I can't believe that happened," I tell Damien in the car as we head to the hotel. "That was the most magical night of my life!"

"It's not over yet," he grins wickedly, pulling me onto his lap.

We make out in the backseat, but don't make it far before the driver arrives at our hotel.

"Come, my little artiste," Damien says as he guides me out of the car. "Let's see if we can't make the night a little more magical."

2 2

ONE HECK OF A GAME

"Maloney, I don't want you to think this game rests solely on your shoulders, but…." Coach trails off in the locker room before the playoffs.

This is our last big game of the season. We win this and we're off to the Super Bowl, something we haven't achieved since the 1970s. The air in the room is tense, all of us holding our breath, hoping that it will give us this victory.

"I won't let you down, Coach," I tell him seriously.

This is the most important game I may ever play in my life. I mean, sure, winning the Super Bowl would be amazing, but it would be devastating to get this close only to see it slip through our fingers.

We run out onto the field, and I remember that I have a whole support squad up there watching me and cheering me on. Damien's arranged a private box for the whole gang. I think McKenzie has even joined them. Harper texted me a picture of her in my jersey, and she looked sexy as hell. Win or lose, at least I'll have the pleasure of her company after the game.

I get in position, more focused than I've ever been in my entire life. This is it. One way or another, this game is going to determine the outcome of our season. I take a deep breath and call our play.

And then it's a whirlwind. My body moves on instinct, and I'm catching throws and making touchdowns without even really thinking about it. My body is on some strange autopilot that my brain is hopelessly behind on. It's all muscle memory from our extensive practice drills. My brain can only communicate two things on a constant loop:

Run faster. Play harder.

We decimate the opposing team in the first half, and I'm so focused during half-time, trying to replenish my electrolytes and keep my head in the game, I tune out almost everything else. By the time we're in the fourth quarter, I truly don't know how it happened. I just know that we got here, and we've wrapped it up pretty quickly.

Our opponents haven't even come close. We're basically just running down the clock at this point. I make one last touchdown, and the game is sealed up. We've won. We're going to the Super Bowl! The U.S. Bank Stadium erupts in cheers so deafening, I have to keep my helmet on just to block it out.

It takes me several minutes just to come back into my body. People are shoving me toward the press corps, and I'm sure that they're asking me questions, and I'm sure I'm answering them, but I'm barely aware of what I'm saying.

"It was a team effort," I make sure I say to ESPN.

"We're really excited," I tell ABC News.

But then I catch sight of Harper. She's running toward me, escorted by a security guard, and her face is radiant. Suddenly, she's the only thing in the world that matters. I catch her easily in my arms and twirl her around.

"I'm all sweaty," I complain, not wanting to ruin her outfit or make her smell as bad as I do right now.

"I couldn't care less," she answers triumphantly, kissing me anyway.

Lights pop in front of my eyes. The press are taking pictures, and this is sure to be front page news in the morning.

"Mr. Maloney, what are your plans now?" asks one final reporter.

"Well, I'm going to take a hot shower, and then I'm taking my girl home."

Reporters clamor with questions, but I'm already guiding Harper away from the field so we can do exactly that. There will be a lot of excitement and activity during the two-week break, and I'm going to have to be on for all of it.

So tonight, I'm going to enjoy Harper as much as I can.

* * *

HARPER

When Rafe won our high school's football championship as a junior, I didn't think I would ever be more popular. It was near the end of our winter quarter, and everybody was congratulating me like I had anything to do with his success. I got endless invites to parties, even though before I was just the weird artsy girl that hardly anyone noticed before. Everyone wanted a piece of Rafe, which meant everyone wanted a piece of me.

It's a lot like that now, only on steroids. I'm so proud of him, and I can't believe he's taking the team to the Super Bowl! I never would have imagined all those years ago that I would be watching him as he won an NFL Championship, leading his team to the biggest sports event in America.

I also didn't imagine that I'd also be dating three other guys, one of whom is at least as famous, if not more than, Rafe is. It's been a bit of an overwhelming few days, to say the least.

I've had to tell my parents that the only thing I'm willing to discuss with them is May because otherwise they'd be blowing up my phone about the championship pictures. Rafe and I seem to be kissing in 4K on every news outlet. I don't see how it's that big of a story, but there are a lot of devastated female fans who absolutely hate my guts.

I actually don't mind that part.

I do mind, however, that plenty of outlets are also still sharing pictures of me and Damien and speculating on the "Mystery Girl Juggling Two Men." I've been called everything from a high-priced hooker to a home wrecker. Some people have wondered if I'm an AI robot that powerful men have created to seem unavailable. That theory did make me laugh. It's creative, at least.

Some sites in Washington state even acknowledge that I'm an artist and that my most recent gallery has garnered some attention. Who knows? Maybe all this focus on my love life will bring even more patrons. That would be a great way to make lemonade out of lemons.

I finally put my phone down and focus on the blank canvas I've been trying to home in on for the last hour.

"I'm creatively blocked," I complain to a restless McKenzie.

"You created an entire series in less than a week," she reminds me without looking up from the piece she's working on. "You're not blocked; you're out of juice. It's okay to take a break."

"I don't want a break!" I huff in frustration. "I want Melody to come back. I want Rafe to win the Super Bowl. I want to work on another series."

"Well, only one of those things is in your control," she answers sweetly. "And if you've got no juice, there's not much you can do about that except search for some creative inspiration."

"Did I tell you Mel's parents called me today?" I can't help but bring up.

She puts down her tools and looks at me in surprise. "Oh, really?" she asks, feigning nonchalance. "And what did Satan and Rosemary have to say?"

I can't help but laugh at this. McKenzie's opinion of Mel's parents is even lower than mine, and she's never even met them.

"I actually missed the call," I sigh. "They called right as Gabriela got to the apartment, and my hands were full. May was a screaming mess, and I just didn't have the capacity to speak to them in that moment."

"So, naturally, you're going to leave it for the rest of the day," she grins. "Maybe that's why you're 'blocked.' They've burdened you with an unnaturally dark energy."

I can't help but laugh. Melody's parents aren't horrible people, I suppose. They're a lot like mine, but even stricter. When Mel told them she was pregnant, they wanted nothing to do with her. As far as I know, they've never even met their granddaughter.

I called them after Melody had been gone for a week. I didn't know what else to do. If I got the authorities involved, they would want to speak to Melody's next of kin, and that's them. Social Services would probably insist that May stay with them.

They didn't answer, which was pretty typical. Calling them was a last-ditch effort anyway. Between Gabriela and my parents, I've been able to keep May well-supervised during the day while I work and at night if I have a date.

Meanwhile, Damien's PI has turned up nothing. The police have no news to share with us, except that the case is very much still open. Which means, basically, nothing at all. Damien even arranged media coverage to help find her. There's nothing TikTokers love more than solving the mystery of a missing girl. Still, it's been weeks, and I'm still taking care of May.

It's not that I mind taking care of her. She's the sweetest baby in the world, and she's finally settled into a good nighttime routine, which has helped a lot with my stress. Damien's completely covered all of her expenses, so that hasn't been a concern. But at some point, Melody has to turn up. Dead or alive. Hopefully alive.

So, imagine my surprise when, three months after she went missing, her parents finally call me. I have no idea what to say to them. Part of me wants to yell at them and let out all the frustration I have about Melody on them. Someone should hear my diatribe. But, at the end of the day, I know that they're just parents who are probably worried sick about their daughter.

"Maybe you're right, and they are the reason I'm blocked," I tell McKenzie. "I'm going to step out and call them back."

"Let me know how it goes!" she sing-songs as I step out into the hallway.

I hit redial on Mrs. Fisher's number and wait with bated breath. She picks up on the second ring.

"Harper, thank goodness!" she says in a concerned voice.

I try not to roll my eyes and bite my tongue. What I want to say is, "I'm not the one who's been dodging calls for the last three months," but I leave it.

"Hi, Mrs. Fisher," I answer as kindly as I can manage. "I'm just returning your call."

"Thank you so much, dear!" she says in such an overly dramatic voice, I decide it's not worth holding back my eye rolls. She can't see me anyway. "Listen, sweetie, we are just so worried about Melody!"

"I am too," I say, trying to hide the bitterness in my voice.

"She's done this before, you know," Mrs. Fisher cuts in as if I didn't speak at all. "But three months is beyond excessive for her. I'm starting to think something terrible has happened to her."

"I am, too," I agree.

"But the thing about Mel that you have to understand is that she lives for the attention," she continues to steamroll. "I mean, really, they're sharing her photo on national news outlets. How much more attention does she really need?"

"Mrs. Fisher," I say firmly, determined not to be spoken over this time. "I don't think she left May with me because she was looking for attention. She was really struggling and–"

"I don't mean to cut you off," she says distractedly, though I'm sure she definitely does mean to cut me off. "My husband just got home, and we have a lot to discuss. Please do let us know if you hear from her soon."

And then she hangs up. What a productive call, I think sarcastically. If anyone is seeking attention right now, it's Mrs. Fisher, and I realize how alone Mel really was. Her parents won't even acknowledge that she has a baby, when mine have been more than happy to watch May. Maybe they'd feel differently if I were the one with a baby, but I don't think so. I think they'd eventually get over themselves.

Wherever Melody is, I hope she knows that she's not completely alone. I just want her to come home safely.

2 3

———

THE CHANCE OF A LIFETIME

"Miss Ward?" an unfamiliar voice asks on the other side of the phone.

I picked up the New York number, hoping against hope that maybe it was Melody, but when the voice told me she was calling from the Metropolitan Museum of Art, I nearly dropped the phone.

"Yes, I'm here!" I say over-enthusiastically.

My heart is in my throat. I have absolutely no idea why they're calling, but I know they wouldn't be calling me if it weren't important. The Met doesn't just call people for no reason.

"My name is Nancy Diaz. I represent Franklin Yates, head curator here at the Met."

I'm breathless, hanging on Nancy's every word.

"Mr. Yates was in Seattle last week and happened upon your gallery exhibition. We would like your permission to move the exhibition here for a period of six months, after which time we will reassess the popularity of–"

"Yes!" I answer before she can even finish her spiel.

I can't believe it! The Met wants to feature my exhibit! This is insane. I try to calm my breathing and wait as Nancy gives me more instructions.

"We'll be sending you some paperwork to sign," she tells me. "If you feel more comfortable going over them with a lawyer, we do encourage you to do so at your earliest convenience. We'd like to get the pieces shipped by the end of the week, with an opening day set for the following Saturday. And we will, of course, pay your expenses to be there on opening night."

Saturday. That's the day before the Super Bowl. Which is on the other coast. Shit.

"Yes, of course," I say, without really thinking about it. "I'll be there!"

The second I hang up, I just stand there in my apartment, phone clutched in my hand like it might sprout wings and fly away. My legs feel shaky. The Metropolitan Museum of freaking Art. The Met. *My art* is going to hang in the same building as Van Gogh and Monet and Basquiat.

I should be dancing, screaming, calling everyone I know. Instead, I sink onto the couch, pressing my palms into my knees. Because even as euphoria crashes through me, it's tangled with dread.

The Super Bowl.

Rafe has worked his entire life for this. This season has been the stuff of legends, especially after he was traded to the 49ers, then traded back. And now, his team is going to the Super Bowl. It's his dream come true.

And I might not be there.

I rub my forehead and groan.

"Why does everything have to happen all at once?" I ask the empty room.

I think about calling Damien first. He's always calm, rational, the one who can talk me through logistics when my brain goes into meltdown mode. But my finger hovers over Rafe's name instead. He deserves to hear it from me.

I chicken out. I toss the phone onto the cushion beside me and curl into the corner of the couch. Maybe I'll just sit here forever and pretend calendars don't exist.

My phone buzzes. Rafe's name lights up the screen like the universe is laughing at me.

I stare at it until the buzzing stops, then curse myself when I see the voicemail notification. With trembling fingers, I hit play.

"Hey, baby," his voice pours through the speaker, warm and cocky all at once. "I just wanted to hear your voice. Practice was brutal today, but knowing you'll be in the stands next week makes it all worth it. I love you. Call me when you can."

I clutch the phone to my chest and close my eyes. My throat aches. He's so certain I'll be there.

I have to tell him.

I press call before I can lose my nerve. He picks up on the second ring.

"Hey, baby," he says warmly.

"Hi," I whisper, my voice uneven.

"What's wrong?" he asks immediately, so attuned to my tone.

"Nothing's wrong," I lie. "Actually, something amazing happened today."

I spill it all before I can psych myself out. Rafe doesn't say a word until I finish, and then he lets out a low whistle.

"Holy shit, Harper," he says reverently. "That's incredible. The Met? That's... God, that's huge. I'm so damn proud of you I could scream. Do you know how insane this is? You're going to be legendary."

Now for the hard part.

"There's just one problem."

"What could possibly be a problem?" he laughs, causing the knot in my stomach to tighten.

"The opening is the night before the Super Bowl."

He's quiet for a beat, and my chest caves in. But then he exhales. "We'll figure it out. Don't stress."

"You mean it?"

"I mean it," he says firmly. "I want you to have this moment. Hell, I'll fly to New York myself if I have to. You're not missing it."

My heart expands so big it hurts. "I don't deserve you."

"Damn right you don't," he teases, making me laugh through my tears. "But lucky for you, I'm crazy about you."

The next few days blur together. There's so much paperwork to fill out and shipping arrangements to make. I'm constantly on phone calls with curators who toss around phrases like "career-defining" and "unprecedented opportunity." Every time I hear the words, I want to pinch myself.

But in the quiet moments, my stomach knots. Because no matter how many logistics I sort out, I can't shake the image of Rafe on that field, scanning the stands, not seeing me. What on earth am I going to do?

As if he can sense my distress, Tomás calls me and invites me out the following night to celebrate. I wait all day in anticipation for it, knowing that no one is as good at distracting me as he is.

His car door opens the moment I reach the curb. He lifts his hand toward me like he's catching the light. He looks unfairly good in a dark suit. His even darker eyes assess me as I walk toward him. He looks hungry, but not for dinner.

"Helena," he says, and my name in his accent is a velvet ribbon around my ribs.

He pulls me against his chest, kisses my cheek, then my temple, then the corner of my mouth like he's drawing a map he already knows.

"You are stunning."

"You are too kind, as always," I tease. "But I did promise you I'd dress up."

A low sound leaves his throat, almost a growl and almost a prayer. "You always keep your promises."

He opens the passenger door and helps me in, like the gentleman that he is. When he gets behind the wheel, he studies me with a cocky smile.

"I can't believe you're going to be displayed at the Met," he says softly. "We are going to toast until the stars get jealous."

Inside the restaurant, the host leads us past clinking glasses and piano music to a corner booth, where champagne is already waiting in a silver bucket. Tomás slides in beside me instead of across, thigh pressed warm to mine. He drapes his arm along the back of the seat, orders in smooth Spanish, and I can feel heat pool low in my belly just listening to him.

"To the woman whose work is going to make strangers cry in New York," he says when the champagne is poured.

The flute is cold in my hand. He doesn't clink. He tips the rim of his glass to my lower lip, pouring a sip into my mouth while his eyes hold mine.

"To your hands," he murmurs. "To your eyes. To your stubbornly kind heart. To your creative spirit."

The words spark through me. All I can think about is getting him into a bed and hearing him say such romantic words in the dark against my naked skin.

"To you," I answer, finally tapping my glass against his. "For standing behind me through every frustrating moment. For always believing in me when I didn't believe in myself."

His hand cups the back of my neck, thumb brushing my hairline. "All I can think about is kissing your sweet lips," he says quietly in my ear.

"So what's stopping you, Profé?" I challenge.

He leans in closer, his warm breath on my face. The kiss is slow, reverent, and celebratory. I taste champagne and feel the promise for more. When he pulls back, I'm breathless, lightheaded, and desperate for much more of that. I only force myself to stay through dinner because he insists I need strength for later.

He feeds me with his fingers, and when my lips close over his knuckles, he inhales sharply. We are both an inch away from snapping, so we try to veer into less dangerous territory.

We talk about the Met opening. He asks about my paintings, which he's only seen in photos. Ever the scholar, he wants to know about the process and the feelings behind them and what brought them to life.

I tell him everything because I know I can trust him with it. I confide all of my frustration and hurt that just came pouring out of me and barely left any room for paint.

He orders himself flan for dessert, which is both infuriating and endearing. I love a man who can appreciate the sweeter things in life, but I've been good all dinner. I haven't grabbed at his pants under the table or whispered what I plan to do to him when I have him alone. I've been good all night, damn it, and he's just prolonging the torture.

"You know," I say, cupping my chin in my hand. "I did leave May with my parents tonight. All night. I don't know how that factors into your flan plan, but…."

I purposely trail off as my foot slides up his leg under the table. He nearly chokes as he calls out to our waiter for the check.

When we get into his house, he tosses his jacket aside, then cups my face with both hands like he's framing me in a canvas.

"I really get to have you all night?" he clarifies.

"I told my parents I'll pick up May first thing in the morning," I assure him.

He kisses me again, and this time there's nothing restrained about it. One moment I'm standing in heels at the door, and the next I'm pressed against the wall, my coat sliding off my shoulders. His mouth is hungry, coaxing until my knees go weak.

He lifts me easily, wrapping my legs around his waist, and carries me to the bed. We tumble onto the sheets, silk and heat tangling. His mouth trails fire down my throat, while his hands roam all over my body, as if he doesn't already know every single inch of it by now.

I arch into him, desperate to feel the heat of him against me. My hands reach up to tug at his shirt, and he lets me strip it off, then pins my wrists above my head, his eyes blazing.

"Tonight you're mine," he growls, thrusting his still-clothed erection against my stomach.

"Yes," I gasp. "I'm all yours, Profé."

His mouth claims mine again roughly, as his tongue slides deep into my throat. I moan into him, my hips lifting, my body begging.

He answers with a low curse in Spanish, then frees my legs so he can pull up the skirt of my dress. The fabric slips away, and he cleanly removes my panties until I'm bare underneath him.

The reverence in his eyes nearly undoes me. "Dios mío. Look at you," he whispers.

His hands trace every inch of me, slow and sure, until I'm trembling. Then he shifts lower, kissing down my stomach, down my thighs, taking his time until I'm pleading for him to take me.

When his mouth finally finds my sensitive mound, I cry out, clutching the sheets. The world narrows to the heat of his tongue, the pressure of his fingers, the rhythm that builds and builds until I shatter.

He rises over me, watching my face as I come undone, and kisses me through it, swallowing my cries. I drag him down, desperate, fumbling at his belt. He helps me, shedding the last of his clothes, and then he's pressed against me, unbelievably hard and ready.

"Now," I beg. "Tomás, please."

He sinks into me slowly, inch by inch, until I'm full, stretched, and trembling around him. His forehead drops to mine as his breathing becomes ragged.

"Mi amor," he groans. "You feel like heaven."

He moves deep and deliberate, each thrust drawing gasps from my lips. I cling to him, my nails digging into his back, my legs tight around his hips. The pace builds, faster, harder, until we're both lost to it, moving together like we've always known this rhythm.

Our bodies move against each other, slick with sweat, the room echoing with moans and whispered words.

I feel myself spiraling again, higher, closer. He feels it too, his hand sliding between us, his thumb circling my clit until I break apart.

The orgasm rips through me, and he follows, groaning my name as he spills inside me.

We collapse together, tangled and breathless. His arms cage me in, his lips brushing my hair.

For a long time, we just lay there, our hearts pounding in sync.

Then he tilts my chin up, his eyes dark and tender.

"Congratulations, Helena," he whispers. "Now you'll show the world what I've known all along."

I smile against his chest, my body sore and sated.

"And what's that?"

"That you are unforgettable."

2 4

THE HOMECOMING

When I open the door two days later, the last person I expect to see standing there is Melody. Her hair is a mess, tangled around her face, and her clothes are wrinkled like she's been sleeping in them for weeks. Her eyes are red, swollen, and wet. She's shaking, clutching the door frame as if it's the only thing keeping her upright.

For a split second, I can't move. I thought she was dead. I thought she had abandoned her baby forever. And yet here she is.

"Harper–" Her voice cracks in half. "I'm so sorry."

The words hit me like a Mack truck. I step aside automatically, letting her stumble in. She's already crying, sobbing from the deepest depths of her soul.

I close the door and press my back against it, my pulse a drumbeat in my throat.

"Where the hell have you been?" My voice is sharper than I mean it to be, but I don't apologize for it.

Her knees give, and she drops onto my couch. She hides her face in her hands, her shoulders shaking.

"I was drunk," she says through a sob. "I was so drunk, Harper. I

177

couldn't stop. After you took May, I went to a bar. I ended up drinking with a crew from a river cruise, and their ship was about to leave, and I just—"

She drags her hand down her face. "I went with them. I stayed drunk the whole time. It was easier than feeling everything I was feeling. I didn't bring my phone. I didn't bring anything. When we got off in Canada, I didn't even have a passport."

My stomach twists.

"Melody."

"I didn't know how to get home," she continues. "I didn't care. I couldn't make myself care." Her voice is raw. "I thought about just staying there forever. I didn't want to live. I didn't want to be a mom. I didn't want to be anything."

Her confession slices through me. She's not making excuses. She's bleeding out the truth. But even so, I can't stop the anger that anger rises inside of me.

"Do you have any idea what you've done?" My words are steady, even though I feel like I'm shaking apart. "We thought you were dead. We thought you were in a ditch somewhere. I've been raising your baby. I've been to the police. Damien put people on it. Everyone has been searching for you."

Her face crumples. She bows forward, rocking with her sobs. "I know. I know. I'm a terrible mother. I'm a terrible person."

I cross the room and stand over her, my arms folded tight across my chest to keep from falling apart. "Your baby needed you. She needed her mom. And you vanished."

"I couldn't do it," she whispers. "I couldn't hold her without feeling like I was drowning. I hated myself for it. I hated myself so much I thought she'd be better without me."

The ache in her voice nearly breaks me too, because I know depression like that is real. I know it isn't just selfishness. It's sickness. Still, there are consequences to her actions. Depression isn't a get out of jail free card.

I kneel in front of her, making her look at me. "Listen to me. You can't ever disappear like that again. You can't just run away from your child. Postpartum depression is understandable, but you nearly destroyed everyone around you."

Her tears drip onto her jeans. She nods frantically. "I know. I swear I know. I'll do whatever it takes. Please help me, Harper. Help me get a hold of myself. Help me be better. I don't want to lose her."

I study her face, searching for lies, but all I see is a woman at the end of herself. Broken. Begging.

I take a long breath. "I'll help you. But you need counseling. You need real help, Melody. And you're going to get it."

"Yes." Her agreement is desperate. "Yes, I'll go. I'll do it. I'll never leave her again, I swear."

Slowly, I stand and go to the bedroom. My chest tightens as I lift May from her crib, her little body warm and soft against mine. She stirs, blinking at me with big eyes that trust me completely.

I carry her out to Melody.

Melody reaches for her like she's holding something fragile, something holy. When May settles in her arms, Melody breaks all over again, pressing her lips to her daughter's hair.

"I'm so sorry, my sweet girl. I'm so sorry."

I watch them together, torn between hope and fury. "She deserves the world, Melody. If you ever pull something like this again, I will fight you with everything I have to keep her safe. Do you understand me?"

"Yes." She nods hard, tears dripping onto her daughter's blanket. "I'll never leave her again. Never."

"Good," I say firmly. "Because I'll be checking on you. Fifty times a day if I have to."

She lets out a shaky laugh that collapses into another sob. "I probably need that."

After a long while, when May's fallen back into a happy sleep, I make Melody call her parents. She stammers through her apology while I stand beside her, my arms crossed.

Then she calls my parents, her voice trembling as she admits what she did. My mom doesn't yell, but her silence on the line is heavy enough to crush bones. Melody promises them she'll get help.

When she hangs up, she looks at me with red, swollen eyes. "Thank you for not giving up on me."

I swallow the lump in my throat. "Don't thank me. Thank your daughter."

After she leaves with May, my apartment feels too quiet. My nerves still buzz. I grab my phone and call Damien.

He picks up immediately. "Hi, little red bird," he says affectionately.

"Melody's back," I say, voice tight. "Call off the search."

There's a pause. "She's alive?"

"Yes. She was drunk. On a river cruise. In Canada. It's a long story."

He exhales sharply. "Are you all right?"

"I don't know," I admit. "I feel like I've been holding my breath for weeks, and I still can't exhale."

"Then breathe," he says softly. "You did what no one else could. You kept her baby safe. You kept everything together."

I close my eyes. "I just hope she means it. I hope she doesn't run again."

"She won't," he says firmly. "Not with you watching."

I sink onto the couch, my exhaustion finally catching up with me. My hands are trembling, but for the first time in weeks, I feel like maybe the ground is steady again. I go into my room and realize I already miss the little girl who'd been keeping me company all these weeks.

To keep my mind off of it, I decide to go through my emails. Lately, my inbox is full of shipping confirmations, gallery logistics, and the occasional spam offer for miracle vitamins. But a new subject line makes me blink twice:

"Feature Opportunity: Your Art, Your Story."

I click it, and my eyes race down the message.

Dear Ms. Ward,

My name is Clara Hendricks. I'm a culture writer for The New Yorker. I saw your work at the Seattle exhibit and was moved not only by the paint-

ings themselves but by the conversations around them. Or rather, the conversations that seem to ignore them.

I'd like to interview you for a piece that focuses on your talent and accomplishments, rather than your personal life. Too often, the media reduces women to who they're dating, particularly when their partners are men in the spotlight. Your career deserves its own narrative, and I'd like to help tell that story. Please let me know if you're interested. Coffee's on me.

Warmly, Clara Hendricks

I sit back in my chair, my mouth open.

A writer wants to feature me. Me, not "the girl in the stands" or "the mystery woman." She wants to talk about my art.

I type back immediately, my fingers flying across the keyboard.

Dear Clara,

Thank you so much for reaching out. I'd be honored to do the interview. Coffee sounds perfect. Let me know when and where, and I'll be there.

Best, Harper

I hit send before I can overthink it.

For the rest of the day, I hum under my breath while I work. Someone wants to hear my story.

* * *

We meet two days later at a cozy cafe downtown. Clara is already at a corner table, notebook open, pen poised. She looks younger than I expected, maybe in her early thirties, with a messy bun that matches mine and a blazer that says "serious journalist."

"Harper!" she greets warmly, standing to shake my hand. "Thank you for meeting me."

"Thank you for asking," I say, settling across from her.

The barista brings our lattes, and Clara gets right to it. "I'll be honest. When I mentioned to colleagues I wanted to write about you, more than one said, 'Oh, the girl dating Raphael Maloney and Damien Blackwood?' That says everything about why this piece matters."

Heat creeps up my neck, but I nod.

"That's been my reality for months. Every headline has been about who I'm with, not what I do. Even my parents–." I pause, swallowing. "They've made it clear they think my relationships overshadow everything else. But my art is who I am. It's not just some frivolous hobby."

Clara's pen moves swiftly across the page.

"Exactly. Gender inequality often shows up not just in the board-room or paychecks, but in narratives. Women get reduced to romance. Men get elevated for achievement. Your story is a clear example."

I breathe in, slow and steady. Her words feel like validation I didn't know I was craving.

"It means a lot that you see that. Because I've worked hard. I studied in Paris. I taught at an art school there. I've got pieces hanging at the Met soon. I've built something I'm proud of."

She leans forward, her eyes bright. "That's the story I want to tell."

For an hour, we talk. I tell her about painting late into the night, about doubts that nearly swallowed me whole, about the moment in Paris when I felt like I had finally become an artist. I tell her about the Seattle show and the gut punch of seeing tabloids plastered with photos of me kissing Damien instead of photos of my paintings.

Clara listens like every word matters. She doesn't press about the guys, except to acknowledge that the fixation on them is part of the problem. I leave the cafe feeling lighter than I've gelt in months.

The article goes live on a Wednesday night. By Thursday morning, my face is everywhere. My paintings, which have been photographed beautifully, are splashed across social media. The headline makes me want to cry in a good way.

"Harper Ward: Artist First, Everything Else Second."

Clara wrote about my brushwork, my use of light, and the way my series captures longing and resilience. She quoted me about Paris, about teaching, about wanting my work to speak louder than gossip.

She didn't once reduce me to "Rafe's girlfriend" or "Damien's mystery woman." She made me an artist in the eyes of the world.

The comments on the article are a mixed bag, though. Some are beautiful. People are saying they're moved, that they can't wait to see my work at the Met. Women thank Clara for focusing on the art, not the men.

Others are not so kind.

She's only getting press because of who she's dating.

If she wanted to be taken seriously, maybe she shouldn't date half the city.

Pretty girl, decent paintings, but let's be real. No Met without Blackwood's money.

I'm about to close the app when I see a comment next to a familiar face.

Harper Ward is a brilliant artist. I'm so glad the world finally gets to see her the way I do. X

It's Lucas. Even after I blew him off and ghosted him, he still only has the nicest things to say about me. My heart warms, and I turn my phone off.

I've nearly given up worrying about what people think of my love life. This article reminds me of what matters.

I've been to Paris. I've taught in a studio full of bright-eyed students. My work is about to hang in the most prestigious museum in the country.

And yes, I'm in love with four incredible men. That's mine. That's ours. No one else gets to define it.

2 5

THE BEST DAYS

Harper

Our black car pulls up to the steps of the museum, and for a moment I just sit there, staring through the tinted window at the glow of the Metropolitan Museum of Art. The banners hanging above the entrance are massive, rippling slightly in the February wind.

Harper Ward: Longing and Light.

My name is on a banner at the Met. My. Freaking. Name.

I turn toward Damien. He's watching me instead of the building, his dark eyes warm, and one corner of his mouth tipped up like he can feel my nervous energy.

"Are you ready to do this?" he asks in a low and intimate voice, cutting through the buzz of my nerves.

"No," I admit, laughing breathlessly. "But we're here and I'm in this gorgeous dress, and people will probably sing my praises all night. Or throw tomatoes at me. It really could go either way."

He squeezes my hand. "All I hear is yes," he teases.

The driver opens the door, and Damien steps out first, offering me his hand like he's Prince Charming in a fairytale. Everything about this feels surreal. Flashbulbs pop immediately, paparazzi shout our names, but Damien keeps his body angled between me and the crowd, his hand steady, his focus on me.

Inside, the museum hums with elegant voices, champagne glasses clinking, and the click of designer heels on marble. My paintings hang in perfect light, each one glowing like a masterpiece.

Guests approach in waves: curators, collectors, and patrons. They speak to me about color and form, about emotion and story, and I try to respond like a professional, but all I want is to pinch myself. Damien hovers close, letting me take the spotlight, stepping in only when someone tries to pull me too far away or talk over me.

At one point, I catch him studying one of the larger canvases, his hands clasped behind his back. I drift over.

"You've seen that one a hundred times," I murmur.

"Never like this," he replies. "Never with the entire world recognizing it as a masterpiece."

Heat climbs my cheeks, and I press my fingers into his arm.

The rest of the night feels like a dream. Speeches are given, there are flashes of laughter, and I take more champagne than I probably should drink. When the evening winds down, Damien takes me outside, wrapping my coat around my shoulders himself.

"You were radiant tonight," he tells me. "I hope you know that."

I smile at him, my heart swelling, and kiss him beneath the glittering city lights.

* * *

THE NEXT MORNING, I'M ON ANOTHER COAST, IN A HOTEL ROOM buzzing with nerves. In a few hours, a car will pick me up and take me to the freaking Super Bowl.

I don't even know how I got from New York to Vegas without collapsing, but Damien was right. The jet made it possible. We landed in time, and now I'm braiding my hair while McKenzie chatters excitedly beside me.

When we get to the stadium, the energy is electric. Thousands of fans roar, team colors flash, and the smell of beer and popcorn are heavy in the air. I find my seat and clutch McKenzie's hand as the game begins.

Rafe looks impossibly focused on the field, his shoulders squared, his helmet gleaming. Every time he moves, the crowd screams his name. My chest swells with pride.

The game is brutal, back and forth, tension so thick I can barely breathe. Then, in the final minutes, Rafe launches a pass so clean, so perfect, it feels like time slows. The receiver catches it in the end zone. It's a touchdown! The Vikings have won the Super Bowl!

The stadium erupts. I scream, cry, and hug McKenzie like a maniac. On the field, Rafe throws his arms wide, his teammates piling onto him. He's grinning so big I swear I can see it from here.

When the clock finally runs out, confetti rains down, and the announcer's voice booms: "Give it up for the MVP—Rafe Maloney!"

My heart nearly bursts. He's the MVP of a Super Bowl-winning team, but he's still my Rafe.

Later, when I finally get to him, he's still in uniform, sweaty, and grinning like he's lit from within. He scoops me up in his arms, spinning me in a circle despite the cameras and chaos.

"You were here!" he shouts over the noise, kissing me hard. "You saw it!"

"I wouldn't have missed it for the world," I yell back, laughing through my tears.

He presses his forehead to mine, confetti stuck in his hair. "I love you, baby."

"I love you too," I whisper, clutching his jersey like I never want to let go.

* * *

THE DAYS AFTER ARE QUIETER BUT NO LESS FULL.

Melody is back in her apartment, and this time, she's really trying. She's gotten May into a really good daycare center, and she's going to therapy twice a week. She's found a good job that allows her to work from home, so she isn't so overwhelmed with everything at once.

And she's not alone.

McKenzie spends a few afternoons there, folding tiny clothes and keeping Melody company. Scott fixes a leaky faucet for her, Tomás cooks meals and fills the freezer, Damien pays for the daycare as well as an evening babysitter and has been helping with her therapy bills.

I'm there as often as I can be, my heart still tied to May in the inexplicable way that only a stand-in mother can be.

One evening, Melody looks at me. May is knocked out against her chest, perfectly content and safe.

"I don't deserve this," she whispers.

I take her hand firmly. "You do. But even if you didn't, she does. And we're all going to make sure she has it."

Tears fill her eyes, but she only nods and strokes May's head.

* * *

THE PHONE CALL COMES ON A WEDNESDAY NIGHT, RIGHT WHEN I'VE settled onto the couch with a sketchbook balanced on my knees.

When my phone buzzes with *Mom* flashing across the screen, my first instinct is to silence it. Ignore it. Pretend I'm not here.

But something inside me says *no*. I've been running from these conversations for months, hiding or bracing for impact. If I want things to change, I can't keep dodging them.

I slide my thumb across the screen.

"Hi, Mom."

There's a pause, long enough that I wonder if she expected voice-mail. Then, "Hi, sweetheart." Her voice sounds tentative and softer than usual.

I breathe through the tension crawling up my spine. "How are you?"

"We're fine." Another pause. "We saw the article. The one about you with your paintings."

My pencil stills against the paper. I don't know whether to smile or steel myself. "Oh?"

"It was good," she says carefully. "Really good, actually. I didn't realize how much you'd done. I knew about teaching in Paris, of course. Sort of. Not the full extent of it. And all those galleries. I had no idea."

The tightness in my chest loosens just a fraction. "That's what I've been trying to tell you."

"I know." Her sigh crackles through the phone. "I think we let ourselves get distracted by everything else. By the men. By the gossip. We thought we were protecting you, but maybe we weren't seeing you clearly."

My throat burns. I stare down at my sketchbook, the lines blurring. "Mom," I say quietly. "I love you. I do. But you don't get to protect me anymore. I'm not a kid. I make my own choices."

Another silence, then a soft, "I know."

They come to visit the next weekend.

I make coffee in my kitchen, moving through the motions like I'm wearing armor. I get essentially the same text from all four men: *Call if you need backup.*

I roll my eyes but smile.

I'll be fine, I type out to all of them.

I wipe my palms on my jeans and open the door as soon as they knock.

Mom steps in first, hugging me tight. Dad follows, awkward with his hands until I lean into him and force the hug. They smell like home.

We sit around the table, mugs steaming between us. At first, we talk about the weather and the new shopping center being built back home. Finally Mom sets her cup down.

"We've been unfair to you."

My heart stutters in my chest.

Dad nods, clearing his throat. "We judged too quickly. We let what other people think matter too much." His eyes meet mine, steady if uncomfortable. "That was wrong."

I swallow hard, fingers tightening on my mug.

"Do you mean that?"

"Yes," Mom says firmly. "We can't say we understand everything about your life, Harper. But we see how happy you are. And we can't ignore what you've built. The art, the exhibits, the recognition. You've done that. No one else."

Emotion surges through me, sharp and overwhelming. "That's all I've wanted you to see. That I'm not just the girl who disappointed you. That I'm more."

"You are," Dad says gruffly.

The words knock the breath out of me. For years, I've braced myself for their disapproval. For years, I've twisted myself into knots to earn their respect. And now, sitting here in my kitchen, I realize something earth-shaking: I don't need it anymore.

I set my mug down, meeting their eyes.

"I appreciate what you're saying. But I need you to hear me too. I can't keep living my life based on whether you approve. I love you, but I'm not going to hide who I love, or apologize for the way I live. Not anymore."

Mom's eyes well, and Dad shifts uncomfortably, but neither of them argues.

"Those are my boundaries," I add, voice steady. "If you want to be in my life, you have to respect them. You don't have to understand everything, but you do have to respect me."

Mom nods slowly, wiping her eyes. "Okay."

The knot in my stomach eases.

Later, when they leave, I stand at the window watching them walk down the street. My chest feels hollow and full all at once.

Rafe calls me first. "How did it go? Do I need to come over there and threaten to bring the wrath of the Super Bowl NFL down on your parents?"

I laugh. "What would that even look like?"

"A lot of angry fans with loud opinions," he answers, and I can hear the smile in his voice.

"It was honestly fine," I admit. "I think things might actually change between us."

The shift isn't instant. There are still awkward phone calls, still moments where my mom's voice tightens or my dad changes the subject too quickly. But there's also progress. They ask about my exhibits. They tell me they're proud.

And I stop clinging so tightly to their approval.

One night, I'm working on a painting at the studio when my phone buzzes with a new article. Photos from the Met are still circulating, but there's a gossip headline about me and the guys. I start to close it, but then I pause.

Because I realize that I'm not angry. I'm not anything, really. There's slight amusement, but nothing else. They can write what they want. They don't get to own my story.

I turn my phone face down and pick up my sketchbook.

26

BEAUTIFUL THINGS

The plane tips its wing, and the island slides into view, all blue water and scalloped beaches and mountains wrapped in soft clouds. I press my forehead to the window like a child who's never seen the ocean before. Scott leans over me and I turn to see his jaw nearly on the floor.

"See?" I tease him. "Wasn't this view worth the flight?"

"Worth every minute of the terrifying certainty that we'd fall out of the sky," he agrees. "I feel like I just opened a door and walked into a postcard."

He threads his fingers through mine on the armrest. We hold hands until the wheels kiss the runway and the cabin breaks into polite applause. It's funny to me, especially with how accustomed to flying private planes I've gotten. But Scott insisted on paying for the trip and refused each and every one of Damien's offers to lend him the jet.

Outside, the air smells like salt and flowers, and it's like I'm breathing for the first time in months. When we get to our resort, a woman in a pink dress loops leis over our heads and smiles warmly as another staff member hands us drinks. It tastes like pineapple and flowers, and something so indefinably warm.

"Ready to see the room?" Scott asks, his eyes crinkling at the corners.

"Lead the way."

He opens the villa door and steps back so I can go first. A wall of glass looks out on a private lanai and a narrow path to the beach. The bed is wide and white and looks ridiculously comfortable. A bowl of mangoes sits on the table beside a card that says my name in neat print.

I step out onto the lanai and let the sound of the water fill me. The waves hush and curl and hush again. The sand looks like it would be warm even at night.

Scott leans in the doorway with his hands in his pockets, his blue eyes a little softer than usual. "It's so good to get away," he says.

I turn and fold myself against his chest. "It is," I say into his shirt. "I'm so glad we have a chance to get away, just the two of us."

His chin rests on my head. "A whole week," he says. "No galleries or farm work to worry about. If you want to paint, you paint. If you want to sleep, you sleep. If you want to eat shaved ice for dinner, I'll pretend it's a balanced meal."

We stand there staring at each other until the breeze makes my hair tickle my cheek and I laugh. He grins and takes my hand.

"Let's get some food and then get in that ocean."

We eat at the bar under a roof woven from reeds. The bartender slides a plate toward us without asking and says, "Trust me." I trust him. The food is hot and a little sweet and disappears while we talk about nothing and everything.

"What are your rules for this week?" Scott asks, licking a bit of sauce from his thumb.

"Rules," I repeat. "I don't want to look at my phone at all, except to take pictures. And you have to be naked at least half the trip."

He taps my glass with his. "I can definitely promise to be half-naked for the whole trip," he jokes, pulling off his T-shirt. "My rules are, I can only check my phone to make sure Rafe and Tomás are keeping our dog alive. And you don't get to make fun of me when you catch me staring at you like I'm the luckiest man in the world."

"I would never do that," I say, then smile. "I absolutely would."

He grins. "I set myself up for that."

On the beach, the water slides over our ankles and retreats again. The sunset is so colorful, my hands itch to paint it. I point at the line where the sun meets the horizon.

"I would never choose that purple for a painting," I tell Scott. "If I did, I would probably scrub it out because it doesn't look natural. Yet here it is, in nature."

"Maybe you will paint it when we get home," Scott says. "Maybe you leave it in because it reminds you of this."

"I like the way you think."

We watch the day sink into the water, and the ocean reflects the light as twilight settles around us. He kisses me, slow and unhurried, and I taste salt and pineapple on his tongue.

We sleep with the doors open. The ocean sings through the night, a steady two-note song. When I wake, the ceiling is pale with morning, and Scott is on his back with one arm thrown over his head, his mouth soft. I watch him breathe and feel my breath fall into rhythm with his.

He opens one eye. "Are you staring at me?"

"I am," I say. "It's a new rule. I get to stare at you when you're sleeping."

"We better put a limit on new rules before we open ourselves up to a whole can of worms."

By midmorning, we're on a path that smells like wet leaves and sun-warmed earth. Birds flick sweet notes into the air. We reach a gorgeous waterfall that looks like it's spilling into a pool of glass.

"I didn't think to wear my swimsuit," I say.

"New rule: We can skinny dip as long as no one is around to catch us," Scott says, and he strips off his shirt with a grin.

"How do we know someone won't stumble on this place and catch us?"

He removes his shorts and wades into the water. "Isn't that half the fun?"

"I'll just strip to my underwear," I say, pulling off my tank top. "And if we get caught, I'm leaving you to fend for yourself."

"I think my farm boy charm and rippling muscles will help," he winks.

He ducks under. When he comes up, his hair is plastered to his forehead, and he shakes his head like a happy dog.

At lunch, we split an oversized sandwich on a shaded bench and argue about who got the bigger half. Later we put our faces in the water just off the beach and follow a sea turtle along the reef.

We dry off in the sun, lying side by side on towels, our toes touching. The wind smells like salt and the faint edge of coconut sunscreen. I point at a cloud that looks like a goose. He insists it is a whale.

Our afternoons become simple and lazy. We take naps and read books. We eat a lot of fresh fruit that's always in plentiful supply. I sketch on the lanai, trying to capture the majesty of this place. Scott dozes in the shade and opens one eye every now and then to tell me I am beautiful when I am frowning at a line.

On the third morning, we try surfing. Our instructor is a woman with copper hair who tucks a hibiscus behind her ear and tells us we'll both do fine. Scott stands easily and rides in like a kid who grew up with a board under his feet. I get to my knees and then perform an elegant slow slide into the water.

"You almost had it," Scott calls proudly.

We go again. I stand for one glorious heartbeat and then sit down very quickly and with great dignity. Scott rides a small wave and jumps off with his arms spread. He's showing off, and we both know it.

On a rainy afternoon, we duck into a small gallery tucked between shops. Watercolors line the walls, the paper wrinkled just enough to prove they're handmade. We walk slowly, shoulder to shoulder.

We buy a small print of black rocks and purple horizon. I imagine it on my studio wall at home. I imagine how it will look when Minnesota goes gray and I need the memory of a wide, colorful sky.

That night we cook in the villa. Scott hums over the pan and plates dinner with a flourish. We eat on the lanai while the last of the rain lifts and a soft pink ribbon appears over the water.

After we wash the dishes, he takes my hand and leads me to the bedroom. We leave the lamps off and let the moon be our light. He kisses me slowly, like the whole night is ours. We wake up in the morning still tangled around our sheets and each other.

The next day, I pick out a few postcards in a shop with shells in the window. We sit on a low wall and write our postcards. I scribble a wave for Rafe and a moon for Tomás and a horizon for Damien, small drawings and smaller notes. Scott rests his chin on my shoulder while I write.

"Tell them I'm hogging you," he says.

"I'm telling them I'm never coming back, and they'll all have to move here," I tease.

"I'll be a surf instructor," he jokes back, kissing my shoulder. "But I don't know what I'll do about the farm animals."

"Oh, I'm sure Damien could sort that all out," I say, and kiss his cheek.

On our last night, we get all dressed up and walk down to the hotel restaurant hand in hand. They're having a special hula performance that I've been annoying him about all week. I couldn't leave Hawaii without seeing a real hula dance.

Scott orders two mai tais and hands me mine with a toast. "To us," he says.

"To us," I say, touching my glass to his.

He watches me for a quiet beat. "Are you happy, Harper?" he asks.

I set my glass down and hold his gaze.

"Yes," I say. "I think I'm the happiest I've ever been in my entire life."

He nods slowly. "Good," he breathes out slowly. "Sometimes I worry that you'll wake up and realize that you don't want all of us anymore, and I'll be the first to go."

I immediately grab his hand and squeeze. "That won't happen," I tell him. "You mean way too much to me to ever let go. I want you in my life as long as you'll let me be."

"I'd let you stay in my life forever," he answers earnestly.

"To forever, then," I say, holding up my glass for another toast.

And I really mean it. From where I'm sitting now, at this amazing restaurant on this beautiful beach, my life is just about perfect. A little over a year ago, I was just trying to make ends meet by any means necessary. I even went on a website where men could pay me for dates, just to keep a roof over my head.

I couldn't have imagined then what my life would turn into. I'm sitting here with this gorgeous man who would hang the moon if I asked him to. Back home, he has a gorgeous farm, and a dog we share. Being with him makes me feel safe and loved.

Also back home is the romantic professor who always encourages me and makes me go after my dreams. He supports me in so many small ways, and in big ways too. He spices up my life with dancing and filthy Spanish words screamed in the throes of passion.

And there's my high school sweetheart, the love who was returned to me. He has become a huge success doing what he always wanted to do, and he's always the first to be my cheerleader. He is my rock and my home.

Finally, there's the eccentric billionaire who has opened up the entire world for me. I could never take for granted how much of my success is because Damien believed in my talent and pushed me front and center. He takes care of me without even needing to be asked, and lavishes me in expensive, over-the-top gifts. But the best part of him is how attentive and compassionate he is.

How could I live without any of them? How could I possibly choose?

The beautiful thing is, I don't have to. At least not now. Maybe not ever.

I have all that I could possibly want in my life, and they're the reason why.

My life is perfect.

ALSO BY SADIE WATERS

Chosen by the Princess: A Reverse Harem Romance,

Realm of the Chosen Book 1

Loved by the Princess: A Reverse Harem Romance,

Realm of the Chosen Book 2

Ruled by the Princess: A Reverse Harem Romance,

Realm of the Chosen Book 3

Realm of the Chosen: The Complete Series

Demon Seer: Ember's Flames Book 1

Demon Hunter: Ember's Flames Book 2

Demon Slayer: Ember's Flames Book 3

Queen of Winter

A Sketch Away from Perfect: The Art of Having it All Book 1

A Palette Full of Lovers: The Art of Having it All Book 2

A Work of Heart: The Art of Having it All Book 3

The One: Four Fae for the Princess Book 1

The Quest: Four Fae for the Princess Book 2

The Crown: Four Fae for the Princess Book 3

Follow me on social media!

Instagram: https://www.instagram.com/sadiewaters/

Facebook: https://www.facebook.com/sadiewatersauthor

Twitter: https://twitter.com/SadieWatersBook

Bookbub: https://www.bookbub.com/authors/sadie-waters

9 798898 710613